Chapter One

Abydos, Egypt. It was as beautiful as Abigail Washington had always imagined it would be. While she had had dreams of arriving at her final destination by boat, it proved to be cheaper to simply take a taxi from Luxor to the last site where she would meet the rest of her team. To think she would be joining a dig for the next few weeks still didn't seem real.

Abigail, known as Aby by her closest friends, had proven to be quite the suck-up to ensure her position on this dig. It was her dream come true. She had been at Professor Sonstroem's beck and call doing research and hunting down leads that led to this very moment. Stepping from the taxi, she couldn't help the broad grin that spread. Everything had led to this moment.

She hadn't bothered with her hat at this point, her sunglasses shielding her hazel gaze from the sun and the prying eyes of those around her. Her sun-kissed blonde hair was pulled back into a ponytail, allowing the breeze to brush the skin customarily hidden. Her skin was darkened by numerous days spent much like she would the next few months, digging under the unforgiving sun. It was the place she felt she most belonged to. Dressed in a pair of khaki pants, she looked like she was born to spend her days on a dig-site.

"Aby!"

This trip wouldn't have been nearly as enjoyable if her best friend, Jasmine Cartwright hadn't been a part of the team. They had spent so many summers digging through muck and mud for some small scrap of something.

Jasmine was her opposite; pale, dark-haired, and tall. It felt as if she towered over her little five foot three at her five foot ten. Her black hair was left to run wild, curls falling in gentle waves about her shoulder. She wore a wide-brimmed hat to help shield her pale skin from the sun. If it followed the path all others had, she would be burnt before the day was through, and it was already late afternoon.

Aby was enveloped in Jazzy's arms, held tight for a moment before they both pulled apart with laughter. This had been their dream, and they were doing it together.

"How long have you been here?"

Jaz shrugged, rolling with everything that was dished out to her, "Only a few hours. I knew you would be here soon, so I held back from going to camp. I wanted us to see it together."

It had become a bit of a tradition for them. They were usually the only women on the digs they had been on. As such, they had made each other a promise to stick close to each other. They had heard the stories of things that happened with women who were alone on these excavations. They didn't want anything to happen to either of them.

Hooking arms together, Aby quickly lifted her backpack onto one shoulder. She was notorious for packing lighter than most women were supposed to. She and Jazz had swiftly learned that it was best to pack lightweight and easy. They didn't want to hold anyone else back, and they had learned quickly that no one took pity on women at a dig-site unless they got something in return.

"We're to be campmates, right? I'm assuming we're sharing tents until you find someone you'd like to spend time with."

Jazz was known for having dig-site dalliances, as they called them. As she had happily informed her friend, they were meant to be nothing more than fun moments between strangers who would likely never see each other again. It wasn't something that Aby participated in. She wanted to immerse herself in the culture and lose herself in the past. There was no judgment between them, though.

Jazz nodded enthusiastically, "We are, as usual. Wait until you meet the others, though. There might even be someone to your liking here this time."

She always said that, and it always proved false, but Aby played along. If there were ever a place that she could believe in miracles, it would be here. The air itself seemed charged with magic that she didn't understand. It only piqued her curiosity all the more. What did the desert hide within the valleys and dunes? Would this be the time she found something that took her breath away?

The campsite where they would be staying wasn't far from Luxor itself, but the man leading this venture believed in being on hand if something happened in the night. The only assumption she could make was he was worried about robbers on the site. Considering they were supposedly working on a site of an ancient temple to Osiris, there was always a chance of gifts to the gods residing within the buried walls.

The thought of being one of the first to step into an unearthed chamber after centuries sent shivers down her spine. She could soon be walking where so many before her had walked centuries before. They would have been reverent with their worship, just as she would be as they uncovered all that was hidden.

"Do you think we'll actually find the temple as Professor Sonstroem thinks?"

Aby had been thinking the same thing. No one knew where the professor had gotten the idea of a temple out here, but, considering the history of the land, it made sense. Abydos was known for being the center of the cult to Osiris. If there were ever to be a place where a temple would be built, it would be here.

"Time will tell, but something tells me this time we may be lucky. If there were ever to be a temple to Osiris, it would be here." She almost felt herself starting to become giddy with the thought. "Can you imagine what it will feel like? We're going to need to make sure we have something on hand to drink in celebration when we unearth the find of the century!"

The laughter that Jazz expelled into the air had her laughter bubbling up. Finding something to drink to celebrate wouldn't be the issue. They usually kept something on hand for such occasions because they believed in being hopeful for a result that led to a discovery. It was almost a good luck charm to have a drink at the ready.

Jazz came to a stop beside a few golf carts with Professor Sonstroem's name on them. Obviously, the camp was close enough that they wouldn't need to ride a camel as they had in the past. Golf carts were reserved for short distances. That also likely meant there would be a few nights those working the dig site would return to Abydos for a night on the town.

Throwing her bag into the back, she let Jazz take the driver's seat. Aby knew she would end up getting them lost. She didn't even bother to listen as Jazz rattled on about who all was at the dig site or the layout of the camp. Instead, her gaze wandered over the expanse of the desert that surrounded them. Egypt was a place that had felt as if it were a part of her. She could almost believe that in a life long passed she had walked these lands herself.

It was a foolish notion and one she had never bother to speak of, but she could never deny the feeling when she came here. It took barely five minutes for the tell-tale signs of their encampment to come into view. Someone had started working on dinner; the fire's smoke curling up towards the sky invitingly. There were many tents at the encampment. The larger ones were towards the center near the fire, while smaller clusters were closer to the desert. That is where they would end up sleeping.

"Our tent is actually closer to the main tent this time. I think Professor Sonstroem remembers us from the other digs before."

She and Jazz were old souls when it came to working the dig circuit. What had started as a way to spend her summers had quickly turned into a passion that had her chasing down any available dig. It meant working with many different professors, but they had both worked with Professor Sonstroem at least three separate times. This was his first dig in Egypt, though.

Getting a tent closer to the heart of the encampment meant that you were held to a higher standard than most. If there were a breakthrough on the dig, you would be one of the first to be alerted. The closer to the heart you were, the more you were trusted. It felt good to know they had risen to this level.

They parked the golf cart near where a few others were. Grabbing her bag from the back, she shouldered it before once more following Jazz. There were a few familiar faces that raised their hands and shouted a greeting as they passed. Sometimes dig sites felt like a family reunion. It was one of the only times they all found time to be together.

Jazz held open the flap to their tent so she could cross. Their tent was how they usually set it up. The cots were on either side of the tent against the long walls, giving them both their own space. A trunk was set at the end of each cot for them to unpack their things. There was a small table with a water jug and a bowl against one corner, and the floor had an old rug that helped with the sand getting where they slept. They wouldn't end up caring before long. Dig sites were dirty, dusty work.

Jazz had taken the space on the left, which meant the right was for Aby. Tossing her bag on top of the trunk, she would unpack later. Right now, she wanted to meet more of their crew and check on what the plan was for tomorrow's dig.

"Lead the way." She grinned at Jazz.

It didn't take long at all to locate the others that would be working closely with them. While some were still in the field or meeting in the main tent to set up who would be working where, most were gathered near the kitchen area, waiting on the food to be ready. Aby recognized only two other people from previous digs, which meant she would have many names to learn before the night was through.

"Hey, guys. This is Aby. She's the last of the ones we were waiting on." Jazz gestured towards her as she sat down next to a man Aby hadn't met before. It was a clear sign that Jazz had already scoped out the options and had decided he was her choice.

"Hey, Abs," one of the men on the other side of the table acknowledged her. Brandon had been someone she had worked with in Greece a couple of seasons before. He had the knowledge and passion that they all aspired to have. The fact that he was here was almost a relief.

Brandon was only a few years old than her, edging closer to 35 if she remembered correctly. His glasses were perched on the bridge of his nose, making his chocolate brown eyes almost the focal point. They seemed to enlarge them to an almost laughable size. Like most of theirs, his skin was sun-kissed. It was a side effect of months spent out in the sun working tirelessly to bring history to light. Sitting down as he was, he looked like more of a classic nerd, but he stood taller than most of them at six foot four. He had a lean build built in the field, and even she had been surprised more than a few times by how strong he was.

He motioned to the man sitting across from him, "This is Baahir Mostafa. He's both our translator and helping in the field."

This was the man that Jazz had decided on, and he was her type. Even Aby could admit that he was attractive. The closest word she could use to describe his skin tone was café au lait. It seemed as if it were made for him. His eyes were so dark they could have been black, but his smile lit up his entire face. He stood as he held his hand out towards her, earning a look of appreciation from Jazz.

"It's nice to meet you. Jazz has been telling me about you. She says you love this land almost as much as I do?"

She laughed, shaking his hand, "I doubt I could ever love the land as much as a local. This land runs in your veins. I could only wish to be so close."

Her words seemed only to impress him more. The moment passed, and she wasn't sure if she hadn't imagined it, after all. Taking a seat next to Brandon, it felt good to be back on a dig site.

"Have we been told where we're working tomorrow?"

While most would frown upon talking shop so soon, Brandon and Jazz were used to her one-track mind.

Baahir was the one that spoke up, "Fred will likely give more information at dinner, but they have us mapping out areas just on the other side of the dunes. From my understanding, it looks like he's predicting this to be an enormous compound. It's going to take a lot of men to unearth this."

Those words had her itching to go to the main tent and look at what had been laid out. That is where most of their ideas and plans would be made and dished out to others. She, like everyone else here, would be expected to put their backs into their work. A vast complex would take more work than if they were concentrating on a small tomb. There would be artifacts to catalog and photograph. They would be expected to write detailed descriptions for every item pulled from beneath the sands.

The Egyptian Department of Antiquities would expect a daily emailed report to keep track of things until they could have their representative on site. While some people might have disliked the idea, they were just as helpful as anyone else in her experience. The amount of knowledge and history they had packed in their heads was impressive. She loved having late night conversations around the fire as the locals told stories she had never read about in all the books she had read.

"What's your opinion on this whole thing?"

He was someone local that she could currently ask. She hadn't gotten the lay of the land yet, but that would happen soon. Even so, it wasn't the same as asking someone who had lived here what their opinion was. They all knew there was a chance that this could be real, but they were also skeptical because Professor Sonstroem seemed to have more information than they usually did when beginning a new dig.

He folded his hands together before him, staring at them before he spoke. It seemed to her that he was thinking over his words before he gave voice to them. Whether it was his intention or not, it had them all leaning in to hear what he had to say.

"There are legends here that the gods still walk amongst us. There are whispers among the workers that they believe these gods are leading Fred. It makes them suspicious of following him, but the money is good."

Aby couldn't help looking over her shoulder as if she expected to see a god standing there waving at her. To think there would be something ancient walking among them, leading them to their ultimate prize.

"Why would the gods want to lead us to this temple?" she asked, turning her gaze back to Baahir.

"Come on, Aby. It's a legend."

Brandon shushed Jazz, watching Baahir just as intently. This was why she and Brandon had hit it off so well before. They could quickly lose themselves to the culture of any country they were in. Start the mention the gods could be walking amongst them? It was the stuff of their fantasies.

This time Baahir glanced around, noting who was nearby them before lowering his voice once more. "Perhaps it is Osiris, and he wants to be brought back into the forefront of our minds. Thoughts have power. To the gods, the less they are thought about and worshipped, the weaker they become."

There was a part of her that was giddy to think there could be gods walking among them. She wanted to meet them and ask questions that could change what the world thought of them. The mere thought of getting a first-hand account was almost intoxicating.

"Don't even think about it," Baahir whispered, narrowing his gaze on her. "If they aren't walking among us and you start searching for them, it could cause a lot of problems for all."

She shook her head, offering him a reassuring smile. "I don't plan on trying to invoke a god if that's what you're concerned about. I wouldn't turn down an opportunity to pick their brains if they do happen to be here, though."

Baahir was on the verge of saying something else when Professor Sonstroem walked out of the main tent, heading towards the canteen. No one dared speak of legends when the man in charge was in their presence. Aby offered him a broad smile, waving to let him know she was there. As far as she knew, she was the last one that was supposed to arrive today.

He raised his hand in acknowledgment before turning back to grab what seemed to be a bottle of water and a snack. If it were anything like previous digs, he wouldn't join them until there was a discovery. They would all celebrate together, but he believed in keeping himself, the foreman, and the site manager separated when work was done. They had to be seen as the people in charge.

The sound of voices carrying as workers from the other side of the dunes began making their way into camp broke up any further conversation. Stories like these were meant to be told around the fire late at night.

Jazz, ever the person to break any tension, grinned, "So what's for dinner tonight? This close to town, we should expect to eat something delicious every night, right?"

The subject change had smiles breaking out around the group as they turned the conversation to something lighter. There was talk of fun things to do around town as they locked in an agreement for Baahir to take them on a tour of Abydos. While Jazz was more interested in convincing Baahir to take her dancing, Brandon and Aby were far more interested in touring the streets and immersing themselves among the people.

Chapter Two

Dinner was a marvelous, friendly affair. It was full of laughter as everyone told stories from past digs. Baahir had his work cut out for him on translating as needed. Most of the men that accompanied them spoke rather well English but struggled over some words. Aby enjoyed learning new words when the moment arose, but mostly the first night was to make friends and build the camaraderie between those who would be slaving under the hot sun for the months to come.

It didn't go late into the night as it would if they made a discovery. They were all too aware that they would be up with the sunrise and work until near sunset. It wasn't as if someone told them they had to go to bed. As the moon began to rise in the distance, everyone split apart to head to their respective tents. The first night was a guarantee that Jazz would be with her.

Neither of them bothered changing into pajamas for the night. It would be the difference between sleeping a few more minutes or having to get up earlier to get ready for the day. They had learned long ago that sleep was a precious commodity that couldn't be wasted.

The one trick that she and Jazz had learned in their years in the field was the ability to shut off at the end of the night, seemingly. Aby could remember the nights when they had first started where the excitement had kept them up until all hours of the night.

This night was different, though. As soon as her head hit the pillow, she found herself pulled into sleep. She wasn't a person that usually dreamed when she slept. It was part of what made this night so different. She found herself kneeling in the desert, the moon shining down to light the dunes surrounding her. While most would have expected it to be cold, there didn't seem to be a temperature.

There didn't seem to be anything or anyone around that would tell her where she should go. Pushing herself to her feet, she spun in a circle before picking a direction at random. Assuming this was the same desert, climbing this dune should lead to the location of the dig.

A few short stumbles later, she was able to get her sand legs beneath her. Walking on the sand was the same as getting used to walking on a boat. It took a few tries before your legs figured out how it worked. Cresting the dune, it was as if the world opened before her.

Stretched below her, she could see an expansive structure. It was as if her dream world had brought to life what she wanted to find. There were two large statues carved at the front entrance depicting Osiris. A couple of men dressed in ancient garb stood near the feet of Osiris, offering their protection to his temple.

From her view above, there looked to be four rooms in total. There was the main and largest building. She could imagine it would be where most of the worship took place. Three smaller chambers were branching off of that one, antechambers that she could imagine were used to store the gifts brought to Osiris.

She could feel an itch in her fingertips to wake and begin working on unearthing this magical place. This discovery wouldn't necessarily change the world or Egypt's history as they knew it, but it would be magical. It was common knowledge that Abydos was the location of the most massive Osiris cult. It would be more incredible if there weren't a temple under these sands. The biggest surprise would likely be the size of the structure. Even she had assumed that it would be of much smaller stature.

Even if this was her imagination, she wanted to run down the dune and see what was hidden within. Would it match what she found during her waking hours? She barely contained her need to race down the dune. As dreams worked, it was as if one step took her practically to the entrance of the temple. The guards didn't seem to notice her existence. It was as if she were apart of their world, but also not.

Stepping towards the giant Osiris nearest to her, she couldn't stop herself from reaching out to touch the structure. It was cool to the touch, reminding her of limestone. Running her hand along the intricate grooves they had sculpted took her breath away. She could stand there all night, staring up at the statues, but she needed to see more before the waking world came back.

There wasn't a door blocking her from entering. If anything, it looked rather inviting. Crossing the threshold, she wasn't sure she could take everything in at that moment. The walls were ornately decorated with the legends they had learned of Osiris. There were smaller depictions of Isis and Horus as well as the story of Seth. Spinning in a circle, she didn't know where to look first.

She wanted this to be real. The mere idea of unearthing the two statues in front would make anyone's season. It would give evidence to what Professor Sonstroem had been saying all along. Maybe Baahir was correct. Perhaps the gods were leading them to this place. Why else would she be having such a vivid dream of a place she had never been?

"Aby!" She jolted awake to see Jazz standing over her, concerned. "You slept through the breakfast bell. I was starting to worry something was wrong."

She could count on one hand the number of times she had slept through the meal bell and needed to be woken up. Those days all happened towards the end of an expedition when they were all exhausted. She hadn't even begun working in the field yet.

Pushing herself up, she offered Jazz a reassuring smile, "I think travel took more out of me than I thought."

They both knew they wouldn't mention this to anyone. Grabbing her boots and her dig-kit, she followed Jazz out to grab something quick before the morning meeting. The sun had just begun to change the color of the sky, reaching out towards them with the promise of heat.

Professor Sonstroem stood near the main tent's entrance, keeping an eye on everyone as they gathered. The workers would meet them closer to the dunes and the excavation site to be given their orders. As this was the first day the entire team would be together, it was customary for their leader to provide them with a rousing speech.

He never seemed to raise his voice, simply raised his hand to get them to go quiet. Aby used to joke that he had to have a secret power because it always seemed to work. Silence fell over the crowd as they turned their attention to their leader.

"It's good to see some familiar faces joining us for the season as well as some new ones. As many of you have heard or guessed by our proximity to Abydos, we believe we have found the location of one of the largest temples to Osiris we have ever tried to find. This is going to be a large venture and will be extremely taxing and hard work."

He motioned towards the dune behind them, that gleam of excitement in his gaze, "Beyond that dune is where we are working. I believe we will find what we're looking for in a matter of days. I hope you are all as excited and ready for a fulfilling season."

Everyone watched him, waiting for him to say something more. Nothing came. A few of them shared glances before gathering their dig-kits to make their way towards the site. It seemed this time it would be best to dive right now.

Baahir took the lead, needing to get to the excavation site ahead of everyone to ensure the workers were beginning. It only made sense for Brandon, Jazz, and her to follow close behind. None of them were above getting their hands dirty in shoveling sand. Even carrying the baskets to dumping piles was in their wheelhouse. The first few days of the dig before anything was found were always back-breaking.

Cresting the dune, Aby couldn't help but pause and look out as she had in her dream. It didn't look the same at all. That should have been expected when one was real and the other a dream. There was a part of her that thought it would be the same, though.

Shaking herself from her thoughts, she moved to follow the others, sliding when the sand gave in their descent. The workers were already gathered near one of the field tents waiting for instruction. Baahir broke away from them and headed towards the group.

"That was a bit of a brief meeting," Brandon murmured once it was only them.

Jazz shrugged it off, though neither she nor Brandon was surprised by this. She didn't tend to look beyond the goal for that day. Day one's goal was always to dig as much as possible and look for what relics might be hidden in the sands.

"It was. I don't think he wants to give away where he's getting the information about this dig. I know there's the joke of the gods helping him, but it's likely a benefactor that got the information by unsavory means."

Jazz turned to where Professor Sonstroem was coming over the dune and laughed, "I don't think he would know what to do with unsavory. The man is practically a saint."

The other two laughed, unable to hide their agreement. Professor Sonstroem had always been notorious for being a straight edge and by the book. While others in their field were more than happy to take whatever they were given, Professor Sonstroem had told many of them that he wanted to lead by example. If he took money from the wrong people, it would be an incentive for all to believe that was how they should behave. He wanted to honor the hunt instead of taking the easy route.

That class had been one of the main reasons Aby had said she would always sign up to work on his dig-site. Shaking her head, she smiled at the other two.

"Whatever his reason, we've got a lot of sand to move, and it isn't going anywhere with us standing around talking. I'm sure he'll tell us what is going on when he's ready."

Neither of the other two argued. They each grabbed a shovel and a basket before making their way towards the dune. It was much like she had dreamt the night before. The dune was built up more and thicker than in her dream, but assuming her mind had been factoring in the past, it would make sense that it would be smaller then.

Baahir waved them over as the workers disbanded and headed towards the dune to being work.

"I have them digging for the moment. If two of you want to work on baskets, I'll need one of you to sift through the sand to ensure we don't miss any pottery or shards that may be hiding."

Brandon and Aby let Jazz take the first round of sorting through shards. It helped that neither of them liked the tedious task while Jazz didn't mind. All-day, they filled baskets with sand and rocks before depositing near those that would look for shards and relics. They would take breaks for water to combat the heat as well as small snacks. Lunch was a straightforward affair as they grabbed premade sandwichs and ate wherever they could find a seat.

They would continue this in the afternoon. The only difference was that Jazz worked on carrying baskets, and Aby sifted through the sand. As expected, there wasn't a breakthrough on the first day. They found some pottery shards that were set aside to be cleaned and appraised, though.

It was just as exhausting as she remembered it to be. She loved every moment of it. When the sun began to set, they packed up what needed to go to camp and headed back. Dinner would be ready and waiting. There wouldn't be any rambunctious stories to be told tonight. The first day was always the hardest. They would eat quickly before tucking themselves into bed.

This is how it would go for weeks to come. They would get up, eat, work in the hot desert all day before returning to camp to eat and sleep. They would wash in the water basins in their tents. Once a week, they would return to town to get a real shower. It wasn't a life for the glamorous. It was real and tiring work.

It wasn't until the afternoon of the fourth day that something happened. Aby was sifting through the sand when she heard a commotion. Glancing up from her work, she looked towards the dig-site before rising to her feet. Her job was here. For that reason, she didn't move towards the noise but waited to hear what was happening.

Jazz came into view, waving frantically for Aby to come over. She didn't hesitate. She barely kept her footing as she raced over the sand to her side, panting.

"What is it?"

Her excitement and happiness were almost palpable. "We've found something. Professor Sonstroem is there now, but it looks to be the top of a statue."

A statue? Those words kept repeating in her had. There was no way it could be the statues she had seen in her dreams. They had just been dreams. Even as she thought it, she pushed past the crowds to approach where Professor Sonstroem and Baahir worked tirelessly to pull more sand away.

The more that was revealed of the statue, the more it felt like she couldn't breathe. It didn't look the same. Years of wear and erosion had ensured that. Even so, there was no denying that it was the statue of Osiris she had seen before. There would be another nearby.

"There should be another one of these close by. The more we uncover of this one and the area behind it, the easier it'll be to locate the other."

Those words from Professor Sonstroem made her blood run cold. How could he know that? Were the gods among them? Her eyes darted around to the people standing nearest her, trying to see if one was watching her. There wasn't anyone noticeable. Even so, she told herself to act as if nothing had happened. Smiling reassuringly at Jazz, she let the excited murmurs roll over her.

The team doubled down on their work, almost seeming as if they were running to deposit the sand elsewhere. It was slow progress even so. By the time Professor Sonstroem called it for the day, they had managed to reveal behind the statue to the first pillar. It wouldn't be far from that to the doors that Aby had walked through the other night.

This was the kind of thing they would celebrate tonight. They gathered up the tools and baskets, joking as they made their way back to the camp. Aby knew that it was pointless, but a part of her wanted to talk to Professor Sonstroem about this whole thing. If he had the same visions as she, they could work together to find the people behind this. Or the gods, as it may be.

She wasn't saying they had to stop the dig, but something in her didn't trust the fact that they both had known of the statues. It took longer than she had hoped. Usually, Professor Sonstroem didn't go back to the main tent on nights when they made a significant discovery. He would celebrate with the team to reaffirm that they were in this together. A win for him was a win for them all. Tonight he went back into the main tent for hours. Most assumed he was going over the shards found in the field to see if it had any details.

Aby paced close to the entrance, wanting to grab him before anyone else could pull him into a celebration. This was a conversation she didn't want to have overheard. She doubted he would like it overheard either.

"Professor Sonstroem?" she called as he stepped out, earning his attention.

"Aby? Is something the matter?"

She hadn't thought of what she was going to tell him when she got his attention. In the hours that she had been pacing, she had been more focused on watching the entrance to the tent than coming up with a story.

"Could I speak with you privately? It's about," she hesitated, not wanting to give anything away immediately. "It's about something I found today."

He seemed confused but motioned for her to step into the main tent now that everyone had left. Stepping through, she crossed to the other side of the tent, wanting to put space between them. He didn't move from the tent entrance, a look of impatience on his face.

She only had a limited amount of time before he would make an excuse and leave.

"I saw those statues!" her mouth fell open over the words that she had nearly shouted, but it got his attention. "I had a dream the other night and saw them. And the temple behind them."

He stepped further into the room; his brow furrowed, "What do you mean?"

For some reason, she felt hesitant now that she had begun. "The first night, I had a dream that I stepped over the dune, and the temple was there. The two statues to Osiris, the compound behind it."

He placed both his hands on the table in front of him, staring down at the map he had spread. He didn't speak for a few minutes, nor did he meet her gaze. The silence stretched, the sound of people celebrating outside echoing into them.

"So," he finally spoke, raising his gaze to hers, "You've been chosen as well. They told me there would be another. I assumed it would be a local. I should have known it would end up being someone with a passion for Egypt like mine."

There was something about the way he said those words as he stared at her that scared her. At that moment, it felt like she shouldn't be in this tent. Especially not in this tent with him alone.

"Fred! You must come to drink with us!" One of the workers called from outside the main tent.

He glanced behind him at the doorway before shaking his head, "We're going to continue this later. The gods want both of us involved in bringing this temple to the world. I want you to work exclusively on the dig tomorrow. No more sifting through the sand to find relics. You're more important than I previously thought."

She didn't move, didn't even breathe until he turned and walked out of the tent. As soon as it closed behind him, her legs gave out, collapsing beneath her. There was no reason for her to have felt that way. The only word she could use was fear.

Grabbing onto the table, she pulled herself up, wanting to get some fresh air to calm her nerves. Jazz, Brandon, and Baahir were sitting around one table, laughing as they passed a drink between them. At a time, she would have been just like them. This time was different, though. She was different now. Whatever was at work in this desert wanted to sink its claws into her. Maybe it would be better for the world if this temple was never found.

Instead of joining in on the festivities, she headed towards her tent. It wasn't much of a safety net, but it would allow her to clean up and try to get her head on straight. The gods wanted the temple to be found, but why? Was it as Baahir had said? The gods gained power from being brought to the forefront of people's minds once more? She washed up absently, going through the motions while her mind spun.

Plopping onto her cot, she tugged her shoes off with a heavy sigh. The more important question was, why had they chosen her? Jazz seemed like a much better fit for being selected by the gods than her. Had the Professor been right? Was she chosen because of her passion and love for Egypt? The sound of voices approaching was enough to have her pretending to be asleep. The last thing she wanted was for others to try to drag her out for the celebration.

She heard the fabric rustle as Jazz entered, followed quickly by shushing. Whoever was with her was just as drunk as she was. It would make tomorrow horrid with the hangovers most of the crew would having. It took a few minutes for silence to fall in the tent. Now that Aby was in bed, she found sleeping tugging her down. She hoped this time she wouldn't have the dreams again.

If the gods were listening, it seemed they had heard to her wish for no dreams.

Chapter Three

Aby wasn't surprised that she didn't sleep well that night. She kept waiting for the dreams to start. It left her exhausted when the breakfast bell rang. At least there would be coffee to help offset her need for sleep. As expected, most of the camp was unusually quiet from being hungover. Being one of the first out at the mess tent meant she could double down on coffee before it was overrun.

Jazz stumbled out a short time later, looking worse for wear. The physical labor would help to combat the hangover, but it would take a while. That was the downside of a night of celebrating. Even if they went to bed at a decent hour, the next day was slow-moving. They didn't tend to get much work done by the time the hangover finally wore off.

"I regret everything. You think I could sift through the sand today?" Jazz asked as she plopped onto the bench beside her.

Aby nodded absentmindedly, remembering what Professor Sonstroem had said the night before. There was a good chance he would follow up on his command last night. While she didn't mind working closely with the statue, she didn't relish the idea of working beside the Professor. She couldn't shake the feeling from last night, no matter what she did.

They sat in silence, both picking at their food for different reasons. Neither Baahir nor Brandon, when they joined them, initiated a conversation either. By noon, they would all be back to relative normality. They could have prolonged their breakfast, but they all knew the drill. The sooner they got to work, the sooner they would feel better.

Pushing up, they began their walk across the sand. Baahir came up beside Aby, offering her another cup of coffee.

"Fred says you're working closely with me at the statue. Do you think we can find the other one easily?"

She yawned, shrugging before she spoke, "I think we can. If we know where one is, we can uncover enough of it to give us an idea of which side the other should be. I don't imagine they would have Osiris holding either his crook or his flail up on the side the other statue will be on."

Baahir nodded, taking a drink of his own. "What happened last night? I've never seen Fred actually assign someone exclusively to just digging before. He normally lets the interns and college students have a turn at everything. What made you special?"

She didn't want to be special. This fell back to the gods again.

"I didn't do anything. I pointed out something to Professor Sonstroem, and he thought I would be of better use closer to the dig." It was a lie, but she couldn't tell him it was because the gods had shown her the same thing they had been leading the Professor. Couldn't say to him that the Professor had decided it meant she was chosen, like him.

Baahir didn't seem to believe it, but he was smart enough not to say anything else. It felt weird to bypass the field tent and head straight towards where Osiris waited to be revealed. At any other time, this would have been a dream come true. Knowing it was only being given to her because of some dream? That took away most of her excitement.

Clambering down into the area that had already been cleared, she approached the statue. She refused to think about anything other than bringing a bit of Egyptian history back to the world. Taking her brush from her bag, she meticulously began to clear away the sand.

She didn't even notice the time slipping by or the workers that came and went around her. All that existed at that moment was her and Osiris. As more sand was removed, she adjusted to the next area revealed.

"It's starting to come together."

She jumped, dropping her brush, when she heard the Professors voice behind her. She had been so lost in her work; she hadn't realized anyone was near her. Putting some space between her and the Professor, she offered a forced smile.

"Yes, it is. We haven't revealed enough to know which side the other statue is on, but we'll get there."

Professor Sonstroem stared up at Osiris before turning his attention back to her. "I don't think the gods could've chosen a better partner for me on this than you. You're meticulous and love Egypt as much as I do."

There was that look again. It was too intimate for someone that was the boss. Offering him a smile, she turned her attention back to Osiris. This was something she could trust. Or archaeology was. Osiris might just have been the root of the problem right now.

The sudden appearance of Baahir had a sigh of relief falling silently from her lips.

Offering him a smile, she motioned to Osiris, "We were just talking about which side we think the other statue will be on. Do you have any thoughts?"

It felt reassuring to have Baahir there instead of leaving her alone with Professor Sonstroem. It was also evident that Professor Sonstroem held Baahir in high regard. She wasn't sure what had happened between them to get them there, but it was a lifesaver at that moment.

They all began inspecting the statue, brushing away more sand to discern which way they should be digging. The workers ignored them, moving around to pull more sand from the back. Their goal was to reveal the temple's entrance. It didn't matter if they found the other Osiris statue or not. What mattered was showing the rest of the temple to the world.

For a moment, she could imagine all the reporters that would want a chance to see this new wonder brought to life. There would likely be cameras and tv crews. She wanted to bring that joy to the world. Somewhere in the world, there was a child just like she had been. Somewhere they would want a sign that this was the path they wanted to take. She had had that moment.

They broke for lunch, eating quickly once more. Everyone wanted to get inside that temple. While she didn't want to be alone with Professor Sonstroem, she did want to lose herself in her work.

"Since when did you become the teacher's pet?" Jazz asked when Aby took a seat next to her. It was surprising to hear her sound so upset with her.

"Are you mad at me?" She would have traded her position with Jazz in a heartbeat. "You hate doing the digging part. You always stick to finding relics in the sand until we get inside."

She took a rather aggressive bite of her sandwich before speaking, ignoring that she had food in her mouth while doing so. "That doesn't mean I wouldn't want the option. You're now his special little pet. Everyone's talking about it. Someone saw you go into the main tent with him last night." Jazz gave her a look that radiated disgust. "You know, I thought we were the same. We could sleep with the other workers, but we didn't touch the ones in charge. It's too dirty and complicated, but I guess it was just me."

The thought that everyone believed that something had happened stunned her. These were people she had worked with before. She had counted Jazz as one of her best friends. If she believed it, everyone else must have as well.

The idea that people she respected now viewed her as a person who would sleep her way to the top was enough to lose her appetite. Gathering her lunch, she simply threw the food away before heading back to the temple entrance. She knew there was nothing she could say that would change their opinion. She had even been in their position once.

It left her feeling so alone. She now had Professor Sonstroem practically breathing down her neck and insinuating that the gods had selected them for this mission and no one else to turn to. Jazz knew her well enough to know she wouldn't try to sleep with the head of their dig to get preferential treatment.

"You're working hard." She jumped at the sound of Baahir behind her. She had assumed he would stick close to Jazz, especially with the rumors spreading about her.

She offered as close to a friendly smile as she could before focusing back on brushing sand from the statue. "I figured there wasn't much point in wasting more time on social situations when we're so close to uncovering something."

It would be a cold day in hell before she would admit that she was hurt by how quickly everyone had seemed to turn their backs on her. Baahir was new to the team. He might have been held in high regard by Professor Sonstroem, but she didn't know him well enough to confide in him.

Motioning towards the lower area, she spared him a glance, "Do you think we'll find the entrance tonight?"

He rocked back on his heels, staring at the exposed wall before him, "I think we will. I think we'll uncover enough to unearth a doorway. Or at least the top portion of it. We probably won't be able to get inside until tomorrow." Flicking his gaze to her, he grinned, "Why? Do you want to be one of the first inside?"

That was the last thing she wanted. If things progressed as they seemed to be, she did not doubt that Professor Sonstroem would like her to be one of the firsts. At that moment, she couldn't think of something she wanted less than to continue to encourage the rumors spreading.

She shook her head, "No, I just want to bring this place to life. Can you imagine how much this could change the world?"

Baahir raised a brow at her words but didn't comment. Even if he believed the rumors, he had too much respect to bring them to her directly. For a few minutes, they stood in silence as she cleared more sand away. It wasn't awkward. It made it feel as if they had known each other for quite a long time.

Her curiosity got the better of her as the silence stretched. "How are you and Professor Sonstroem so close? Why does he seem to defer to you on decisions made in the field?"

Initially, she had assumed that Professor Sonstroem thought he had more experience when it came to the workers. With so many things coming to light at this point, she didn't want to assume. As far as she knew, it could mean that he also had been blessed by the gods in this case.

Baahir studied her a moment before grinning, "I could keep you in the dark. It's not as if you could find out any other way. The truth is," he paused, glancing behind him to ensure no one was listening. "The truth is I'm the one leading Fred to this temple. I'm not the gods I told you about, but I'm of their loyal subjects. It's time for them to have a rise in power again."

She dropped her brush, scrambling to put space between them. Her actions only seemed to make him laugh. It wasn't fear that had her wanting the distance between them. It was the idea that, once again, the gods were interfering in her life. This dig felt more and more dangerous by the moment.

"You don't have to be afraid. I know Osiris showed you the temple as well. Fred was lamenting the fact that he didn't have a female counterpart. Osiris wanted to give him someone worthy. It wasn't until you arrived that he made up his mind. Jazz was the other option. I don't imagine she would be handling this as well as you are."

She stared him down, chewing on her lower lip in her nerves, "I don't want this. I don't want any of this."

He shrugged, "The gods know what's best for each of us. This will be good for you."

She was saved from further comment as the workers returned from lunch. Everyone was too focused on uncovering the entrance to notice the tension between the two standing in the shadows of Osiris. Aby suddenly didn't want to be here anymore.

<u>Chapter Four</u>

Aby did her best to stay busy and to stay away from both Baahir and Professor Sonstroem. It was easy to avoid everyone else since they were avoiding her. What had been the thing she was looking forward to most was now the thing she was dreading. When the workday was over, she walked back by herself, keeping her distance from the others. It was the same when she grabbed her dinner. She took her food and walked to the edge of the camp, tuning out the voices behind her.

This reminded her of her first few digs before she had met Jazz. She had always been a loner and kept to herself to ensure she didn't upset anyone. It helped so much. She thought the last thought sarcastically. She shouldn't have ever worried that she would upset someone because she tended to take charge and lost herself to her passion for the dig.

Here she was years later, right where she had started. She made quick work of her food, not wanting to linger even here. It seemed pointless to go back to her tent. If she could hold out until after Jazz went to bed, she wouldn't have to endure the snide comments.

She could feel the stares as she returned her dishes to the piles of those that would be washed later. There was no indication from her that she noticed. She cast a smile at the person taking her dishes before turning back to walk into the desert. It was common knowledge not to wander too far from the camp, especially with night approaching. The distance always helped, though.

Right now, she just wanted to be reminded of why she chose this profession. Egypt had been her obsession since she was a child. She would stay up all hours of the night watching specials on digs taking place. Each tomb unearthed felt as if it reached out to her very soul and was a part of her. Her first dig had felt like coming home. Every time a dig in Egypt opened up, she was there.

A part of her now wondered if that wasn't what led the gods to decide she was what they wanted. Taking a seat at the top of the dune overlooking their dig, she sighed heavily. She didn't want this entire experience ruined. It was just escaping her at that moment how she would make that happen.

This had been the chance of a lifetime. That had been her original mindset. Now, she just wanted everything over. She couldn't just leave, though. That would paint her in a bad light. It would be nearly impossible for her to get into another dig. If she had been thinking of pursuing another career path, she might have been willing to throw it all away. Dig sites were the place that she felt alive. She couldn't throw it away.

"There you are."

She jumped, unable to get her footing under her with the sand, as Professor Sonstroem approached.

"I was looking everywhere for you. I had hoped you would join me for dinner, but I've been told you already ate."

She nodded, finally able to stand. "Yes, sir. I ate with everyone else. Is there something I can do for you?"

He gave her a soft smile, taking a step towards her, one that she echoed as she took a step back. "You don't need to call me sir. Please, call me Fred. The gods have decided we're perfect for each other. We don't need to be formal."

She gulped, shaking her head, "I don't care what the gods claim they have decided for me. I make my own decisions. I'll work on this dig with you, but there's nothing else between us, Professor."

He frowned, his brow furrowing in confusion. Silence stretched between them. The longer the silence reigned, the angrier he seemed to become. Had he believed that she was meant to be his simply because a god promised him a female counterpart?

"You are mine." He seethed, gritting his teeth and clenching his fists at his side.

That feeling of danger washed over her once more. All she knew at that moment was that she needed to put space between herself and him. He took a menacing step towards her, reaching out as if he meant to grab her. She tried to evade, but the sand only seemed to cause more of a problem. It caused her to lose her footing, sending her tumbling down the dune to the dig site below.

When she came to a stop, she had no idea how close or far she had fallen. More importantly, she had no idea where Professor Sonstroem was. That was the more important matter. Struggling to her feet, she made a note of the pain on her left side, but it wasn't something she could worry about right now. She needed to find a way back to the camp without crossing paths with the Professor.

"Aby! Stop! Let's talk about this!"

Even hearing him yelling after her had her doubling down on her effort to get away. The temple wasn't an option. The entrance hadn't been uncovered yet. She could try to loop around and scramble back up the dune on the other side, but he had more of a chance of catching her. His strides were longer and he wasn't injured.

She didn't waste energy by calling back to him. All her focus was on putting more distance between them. She dashed to the end of the temple that was revealed, hoping to hide her progress in the shadows. Before she could get too close, Baahlr stepped out, raising a brow at her. It was as if he had materialized from nowhere.

"Now, Aby. I told you the gods know what's best for you."

She screamed, turning away as quickly as she could. This let her see just how close the Professor had been to her. They were working together to try to corner her. That left her with one choice. Turning from them both, she raced into the desert. Typically, she never would have even considered this as an option. Desperate times called for desperate measures.

"I wouldn't go that way!" Baahir called after her.

If anything, that only encouraged her to head further and faster into the desert. It could have turned into a death wish, especially if she didn't manage to find her way back before it got too cold. Staying here and letting them catch her could prove even worse, though.

She couldn't guess how long she ran or for how far. All she knew was one minute she was running; the next, the ground seemed to give way under her. She screamed again, flailing for only a moment before the sand sucked her beneath. She didn't know if she had passed out from fear, pain, or if there had been a momentary lack of oxygen from the sand swallowing her. When she blinked her gaze open, she found herself in a modest but elegant chamber. The markings on the wall indicated that this was a temple.

Pushing herself to her feet, she approached the wall nearest her, running her fingers over the hieroglyphs carved there.

"Temple of Noor. Is this a temple to Amun Ra?"

A slow clap behind her had a gasp tumbling from her lips as she turned quickly, pressing her back against the wall. Was there a chance Baahir or the Professor had caught up to her already?

"Bravo. I must say I didn't think you'd find this place. I'm impressed. I can see why Osiris thought to steal you to be one of his obedient children."

The man that walked forward was neither of the men she had been running from. She had no idea what to make of him, though. He was a walking Vogue magazine cover. His hair was long, a mixture of black and browns that he had pulled back in a stylish low ponytail. While it should have made him seem like a vagabond, it only added to his elegance. His skin was the most beautiful charcoal color she had ever seen. Piercing golden eyes stared out at her with a playful gleam. It was as if he knew a joke and was waiting for everyone else to catch up.

The most peculiar thing about this entire situation was how he was dressed. He was dressed in a business suit. It was tailored perfectly to him and only hinted at the muscular frame that resided beneath. To put it simply, he was probably one of the most attractive men she had ever seen.

"Who are you?"

He chuckled, motioning to the walls around them, "This is my temple. You should know very well who I am."

She looked back at the hieroglyphs she had been reading before slowly turning her gaze back to him. Another god? She thought she had been putting enough distance between her and the other temple only to fall into the hands of another god. At least this one had decided to appear before her. Osiris had only sent one of his lackeys to do his dirty work.

"You're… Amun Ra?"

He grinned at her, "Bingo. It seems like you've found yourself in a sticky situation. I just so happen to have a solution for you. If you have the bravery to accept my challenge."

More gods were playing games. It was strange to think about how quickly she had come to accept this as a part of life. Osiris was trying to pawn her off as a bride to her professor. The least she could do was listen to what Amun Ra was offering her.

"I'm listening."

His grin turned into a full-fledge smirk. "I knew you would be fun. Now, let's get down to business." He approached her finally, maintaining his distance. "My offer allows you an escape from this situation. It's your choice if you ultimately end up back here. You see, I think you can be an asset, but you're not quite there yet. I have the power to send you to… other locations where you will be expected to learn lessons. These lessons will only make you more powerful. It'll bring you closer to unlocking your potential. When you've finished your last lesson, you'll return here. Where you go from here will be your choice. You can stay in this location and face what lies ahead, or you can return to any of the other locations and live out the rest of your days."

She blinked in confusion, running over what he was offering her. Other locations? That didn't make sense. How would other locations change her present?

"Do you mean other worlds?" It was a stretch to ask, but she didn't feel like beating around the bush anymore. The worst that could happen was he would laugh at her for even suggesting such a thing.

He nodded, "Other worlds. Other realities. They're just words. You'll be far from here. Far enough that Osiris nor I can touch you. You'll be on your own."

She could be traveling to other worlds. That mere sentence had her scoffing in surprise. It would be a chance to see more. Just thinking of all she could learn by going to other worlds nearly had her jumping at the option. This was a god that was offering her this chance, though. There had to be conditions.

"What's the catch? Why would you want to help me?"

He nodded thoughtfully, "I'm sure others have told you that the gods mingle in your world. We don't have the power that we did before. The more people that believe in our mere existence, the more power we have. This, though?" He grinned with mischief, "This is because Osiris wants you so badly. We're quite competitive between ourselves. As you can see, he built his temple close to mine. Our rivalry hasn't died yet."

She was caught in a pissing match between two gods. How did a girl get so lucky? When push came to shove, though, she didn't have much of a choice. Amun Ra had once been the most worshipped god in Egypt. It made sense that the gods would want to spice up their immortality. To them, mortals lived such finite lifespans. They were like ants in their eyes.

"The only catch is that I'm on my own if I accept, and you're only doing this to get back at Osiris?"

She was so calm. She could hardly believe she was talking to the embodiment of a god.

He shrugged, not answering her question. The implication was there was something he was hiding, but at that moment, she didn't care. There was no going back.

"Let's do this then. Do I get a heads up on what lessons I'm learning?"

He shook his head, "Part of the fun of life is figuring things out. There will be hints. Don't worry about that. I won't let you wander around completely blind, or I'll never win."

It was all about winning for him. She couldn't say she was surprised.

"What about clothes? Essentials? Or at least currency to spend in these other worlds? I think we both want me to fit in if I'm to complete these lessons quickly."

The question seemed to catch him off guard but had him pausing thoughtfully. "That's a valid point. I had just assumed to let you go on your own and figure it out. You've got a brain, though. How about this? When you land in each reality, there will be a pack nearby for you to find. It will have clothes, essentials and some currency. I don't want you completely beholden to the world. You're stronger than most anyway. It would likely only intimidate them."

He couldn't make it easy. Even so, she would take what she could get.

"Then I believe we've reached an agreement. I'll travel forward and learn the lessons you've laid out. When I return, we'll go from there. Deal?" She held her hand out, ready to shake on the agreement.

Amun Ra looked at her hand before shaking his head. "No need for such human pleasantries. Your word is good enough." Stepping to the side, he motioned to an archway that stood in the middle of the room. "This is your entrance. In a moment, it will fill with light. That is the portal activating. I wish you luck, Abigail Washington."

Of course, he knew her full name. It was a little trite that the Temple of Noor used light to activate a portal. If she remembered correctly, Noor was another name for light.

She didn't bother trying to continue their conversation. There wasn't anything else he could tell her. She should have been more nervous than she was. In a way, it felt as if she were resigned to the path she was taking.

A flash of light filled the room, momentarily blinding her before it settled to a steady level.

"Your ride is here."

She didn't bother to spare Amun Ra a glance as she approached. It was now or never. Remembering Baahir's words, she trusted that Amun Ra knew her true worth, even if she couldn't see it at that moment. She took a deep breath, staring at the portal before her. If there was one lesson she had learned in life at that point, it was not to look back at the past. Her only option was to move forward. She would throw herself into this the same way she had thrown herself into everything up to this point.

Chapter Five

Retaking a deep breath, she stepped through the light. She had been expecting some crazy sci-fi tunnel that would yank her through to another location. Instead, it was like stepping through a doorway. One moment she was in a temple in Egypt; the next, she was standing in an oasis on the other side. Glancing around, it seemed as if nothing had changed. If she was correct, she was still in Egypt.

A quick search of the oasis showed that she was alone. If there was ever a time that she would give thanks to a god, it was at that moment. He had given her a chance to bathe before she attacked this next level. Knowing there was no one around was all the incentive she needed. She quickly located the pack that Amun Ra had promised her, bringing it closer to the water to get dressed quickly once she was done.

Stripping, she gasped when she stepped into the water. It was colder than she had expected, given the harsh sun beating down from above. Even so, it had been days since she had done anything more than rinse off from a bowl. Dunking under the water, she couldn't think of anything more impressive than how clean she felt at that moment. Days of sand, grit, and sweat washed away. This alone would make the entire experience worth it.

Knowing an oasis in the desert was hardly a well-kept secret, she made fast work of cleaning herself. The last thing she needed was for someone to walk in on her bathing and get the wrong idea. The clothes she had been left were going to take a moment to get used to. It was not what she wore in the desert, but she could admit that it left her feeling cool. It wasn't the transparent linen of a wealthy woman, but that was more comfortable to her.

It reminded her of a sundress, though in sheath form. A single strap held it in place over her shoulder. Jewels were given in the form of bracelets and a collar. It was far more expensive than she had ever owned in her life. Sandals were assigned to cover her feet from the sharp sand. She packed her clothes into the bag. While she wouldn't likely have any use for them while she was in this world, she wasn't going to leave them behind.

The downside of this, though? She wasn't sure which direction she should head in to find civilization. Moving out of the shade of the oasis, she found herself spinning in a circle. Nothing. There weren't even tracks in the sand for her to follow.

There were dunes as far as she could see. While it didn't necessarily mean she was in Egypt still, it let her know she needed to find civilization. Staying out in the desert too long would cause lasting damage. With no sign of where to go, she started walking towards the nearest dune. If she climbed to the top, she might get an idea of which way to go.

It took her a few moments to get to the top. Admittedly, part of the reason was getting used to the new attire. Reaching the top of the dune with only minimal slipping in the sand, she took in the view. It was quite an expansive desert. It looked like she had been teleported the same distance from civilization in this world.

Turning in a slow circle, she studied the horizon closely. It was in the hopes that she would see which way to go.

"There you are!"

She jumped, pressing a hand to her chest to calm her heart. This was the second time that someone had tried to scare her at the top of the dune. At least this time, she hadn't fallen down the other side.

Turning, she expected them to realize she wasn't who they were looking for. Instead, she got a shock. The man standing mere steps from her looked like Brandon. Not in coloration, but the structure of his face and height. He seemed to be a native, in this case. His skin was deeply sun-kissed, almost caramel in the late afternoon sun. His eyes were so brown; they bordered on black.

"Are you looking for me?" she questioned.

Brandon, for lack of a better name, gave her a perplexed look, "Yes. You said you wanted to scout the oasis. We stood guard while you did so. Are you feeling all right?"

Apparently, she hadn't been brought as someone new to this world. That was going to take some getting used to. She didn't have any of the memories that these people would have with her. Even so, she offered him a reassuring smile.

"I didn't realize you all would be looking for me. That's all."

He inclined his head, though she didn't think he readily agreed with her. It was more as if he simply didn't want to bother with arguing. Did that mean she was someone of power here? The implication was there.

Allowing him to lead the way, she followed him back to where she was greeted with her first surprise. She had assumed when Amun Ra had said he would send her to another world; he had just meant to the past. The clothes she had found seemed to confirm that.

However, the animals that they were supposed to ride were most certainly not of this world. They had the same general characteristics as camels. The coloration and fur covering most of their bodies matched. There were humps on their backs as well. The most significant difference was that these creatures had wings. Fully feathered wings.

"If you're done scouting the oasis, we should get back. It'd be best if we were indoors before nightfall."

That was a strange timeline. Did something happen after dark? She didn't want to ask, though. It seemed like something she should have known if she had been of this world.

"Will we make it back in time?" Another voice drew her attention.

There was another woman mounted on the creatures she had seen before. It took her a moment to realize this woman closely resembled Jazz. The difference was, again, a darker skin tone, and she was a little fuller figured. The Jazz she knew had lived a hard life and spent many years not having enough food. This woman hadn't known such hardships. It was in the way she held herself and interacted with those around her. There was a confidence there as if nothing could go wrong in the world. She could have been reading the entire situation wrong, though.

Brandon seemed to consider this, looking up at the sky. "I think we'll make it. It's going to be close, though."

Jazz shook her head, shivering at the thought of being out after dark. It only piqued her curiosity all the more.

"Even if we're a little later than usual, they won't close the gates. We've already made a sacrifice for this cycle. They should be appeased." He scoffed, clambering onto his mount. "You would think the gods would be content with all they've stolen from us."

Now that would need some unpacking. She would try to see what she could find out once they were back where they were going. Clambering onto her mount, she motioned for Brandon to take the lead. It seemed familiar since he didn't protest or give her a strange look. They took to the sky, flying in a triangular pattern. That alone would have made this journey worth it.

A part of her wanted to lean her head back, throw her arms out, and shout to the sky. The wind tugging at her dress and whipping her hair about her face was a sensation she had never felt before. Her life was in the hands of the beast beneath her. She had never given much thought to the idea of flying like this before. It wasn't an option in her reality, but even the idea of paragliding hadn't held appeal for her.

It felt as if they were racing the sunset. Brandon and Jazz rode low on the creatures, making themselves parallel to their mounts. There was enough for her to mirror their movements. Whatever had them scared of being out after dark was enough. Until she knew what she was dealing with and figured out her lesson in this world, she would stick close to these two. It couldn't be a coincidence that they looked like people from her world.

It took them a little longer than sunset to reach their location. Brandon led them into a large complex that was mostly buried in the side of a dune. She had been expecting a massive civilization, but it felt like that wasn't the case here. Again, she couldn't ask any questions. It would give everything away.

Landing quickly, all three dismounted before handing the reigns to attendants waiting. None of these people reminded her of anyone she had come across before. It seemed Amun Ra had lined up for the people she was around the most to look like people she knew.

"We need to go tell Akar what we found. That oasis could help get at least water and some vegetation." He started heading into the structure, once more leading the way.

Aby kept close at his heels, letting her gaze take in everything around her. This wasn't how Egypt would have decorated. The walls of these tunnels were rough and blank. Perhaps it was because it led from a lower entrance that servants worked? Would the décor change as she climbed higher into the complex?

Brandon didn't go much higher into the complex. Taking a left turn, he led them down another set of hallways. These also weren't decorated. Maybe Amun Ra had been telling the truth. This world closely mirrored ancient Egypt, but there were a lot of fundamental differences. A big one being the gods were accepting sacrifices and forcing people below grounds.

He stopped at a rough wooden door, rapping on it until he was given the clearance needed to enter. The man standing by a large table that had been converted into a map barely acknowledged their presence. That was why it took her a few moments longer to realize that he looked like Baahir. They could have been twins. Everything was the same; hair color and style, eyes, facial structure. It seemed Baahir had been telling the truth. He was only a servant to Osiris.

It didn't seem likely if he had been the embodiment of Osiris, he would have been able to exist in this world as well. If she found someone that looked like Amun Ra, though, all bets were off.

"What did you find?"

Brandon nudged her forward as if she was the ring leader of their trio. She wasn't going to do anything to set off any warning bells.

"We discovered an oasis within a few hours ride of here. The water was fresh and untainted. Cool despite the desert heat."

Baahir regarded her closely as if he were trying to see if she were lying. "No sign of the gods there?"

Brandon shook his head at her side, "She scouted out the interior of the oasis while we stood guard outside. No tracks were leading into the oasis. It seems a good chance we found it before they could."

"This means we have a limited timeframe to harvest what we can before they take over. I want you to organize a team to go there tomorrow. Get everything you can."

Brandon nodded, pressing his fist to his chest before bowing. Aby wasn't sure if she was supposed to follow suit, but Jazz didn't either. Taking her cue from there, she slowly backed out of the room with the others.

"You're going to have a long day tomorrow," Jazz grumbled. It seemed some personality quirks translated across worlds too.

He nodded in reply, running a hand roughly through his hair, "I need to gather whoever we have available tomorrow and make sure all the beasts are prepped."

It seemed as if they both knew all too well what had to be done. She felt like she was holding them back.

"Just tell me what I can do to help."

Jazz and Brandon exchanged a look before Brandon spoke. "Scouting missions are one thing. This will be extremely dangerous. At any moment, we can run into the gods. There isn't a guarantee you'll return here."

"And? I can help. You said yourself you need everyone you can get."

He shook his head, taking a deep breath as if to calm his anger. "You know the law. You aren't of an age where you can go on these missions yet. Your father hasn't even married you off, so you can help ensure future generations. Until you've given the kingdom your two, you are only allowed to go on scouting missions. Even that took a lot of convincing."

Her two? She wasn't some mare waiting to be allowed to give birth when a stallion was chosen for her. She was here for a reason. Something told her that reason involved going out into that desert tomorrow.

"I'm going. And that's final. You can argue until you're blue in the face, but I think we both know I'll get my way in the end."

She didn't bother to give him a moment to answer. Turning away, she marched down the hall they had come up. As far as she was concerned, the conversation was over.

Chapter Six

Aby wasn't sure what kind of power she had in this world, but it was enough to get her on the recon mission the next day. She had assumed there would be some sort of argument against it. Perhaps it fell to the power her family had. Whoever her father was, he seemed to strike fear in those that opposed him. From what she had seen, most women her age already had provided their two children.

There didn't seem to be any written history or traditions. At least that she had found. The only way she was going to get answers was by listening. Asking questions was out. It would give too much away. People thought she was meant to be here. She couldn't expect them to believe that she had come from another world. Least of all brought there because of a god.

She had an idea to use this recon mission as an opportunity to learn more about what they feared. Who were these gods? Why were they so worried about them finding the oasis before they could take what they wanted? What gods needed vegetation and water? There was something strange going on. She did love a good mystery, though.

They met at the caverns just before dawn. The sky was beginning to lighten as they loaded down the flying camels and prepared for their mission. Whoever these gods were, they had them too scared even to step outside before the sun had peaked over the dunes.

There were only twenty people that had been chosen for this mission. Most of which were men. There were three women in total. Jazz was an easy guess. Aby wondered if there was something between her and Brandon, but Jazz had stated she had already had her two children. It hadn't been with Brandon. From her observations, it seemed as if the women were paired with much older men.

She could only assume there was a system that decided who got a wife and children and when. In her opinion, Brandon deserved to have a family of his own. It seemed it was something he wanted as well. Was that her mission? Something told her it wasn't.

Once again, they all followed Brandon, each clambering onto their respective creature. She doubted flying would ever get old. It was chillier than it had been last time she flew, but she loved it either way. It seemed to take no time at all to reach the oasis. Brandon had them circle before finally touching down.

The oasis looked the same. It seemed whatever gods they feared hadn't found it yet. She climbed down with the others, gathering their bags and baskets to begin. They split into two teams. There were more that headed to the water first, filling bladders with fresh water. The rest went through the vegetation and grabbed anything that could be edible or replanted for their use later.

The work rivaled that of working on a dig in the summer heat. Even with the comfortable clothes she had been given, she felt as if she would waste away under the sun. They took breaks in shifts. Brandon wanted to make sure they had someone working around the clock. It would ensure they finished more quickly. He also had someone stationed as a guard. He assumed that someone was going to try to sabotage them. These gods, presumably.

When her break finally came, she thought she would break down in tears. The downside was she hadn't gotten any information on what her mission was. She had more blisters than clues at this point. Walking away from where everyone was working hard, she wanted that moment of peace before forcing herself to continue the manual labor. It was as close to peace as she had felt in a long time. The distance between her and the others nearly drowned them out.

Straying close to the edge of the oasis, she couldn't help but wonder once again what her mission here was. Snacking on the fruit that Brandon had given her, she could admit to herself at that moment that she would have chosen this world if she was given a choice right now.

A rustling in the foliage behind her had her turning. Was someone coming to find her? She hadn't been gone that long, had she?

"Hello?" she called out, moving towards the noise cautiously.

The rustling stopped, the brush going still. It was too still. Someone was hiding in there. Again, the question arose as to why.

"I won't hurt you. You can come out. I promise I'm nice."

All reassuring things, but it didn't seem to be working. When in Rome, right? Crouching down to make herself on the same level as whoever was hiding, she slowly approached. She would treat this as if it were a stray dog. Approach with caution, keep her voice pitched low and nonthreatening. The goal was to get whoever was hiding to come out.

She didn't know how long she would have before Brandon came looking for her. It felt like it took an eternity before she found a pair of caramel orbs peeking at her through the green foliage. They looked like young eyes, still innocently gazing at the world. There wasn't any threat there at all. Offering them a smile, she held out her hand, offering the last of the fruit that she had.

This seemed to be the final straw. Slowly, matching the speed with which Aby had been using, a young girl emerged from the foliage. If she had to guess, the girl couldn't have been more than sixteen. She accepted the fruit, watching Aby closely as she smelled it before taking a cautious nibble.

"Are you lost?"

The girl shook her head slowly before finally speaking. Her voice was husky, as if she had spent far too many days screaming in pain. There weren't any signs of abuse that Aby could see, but that didn't mean anything.

"Aren't you scared of me?"

That was an odd question. It only made Aby grin at her, though.

"Why would I be scared of you? You're like me."

She shook her head, "I'm not. That's why I'm out here while you're tucked away in that prison. You can have children, or they would throw you away as well."

Throw her away? Had this girl been from the complex before?

"I don't understand. Did they throw you away? How long have you been out here?"

The girl paused thoughtfully before holding up a whole hand. She had been out here for five years. She claimed it was because she couldn't have children, but she would have been too young to have them at that age. Or most girls would have been.

"I'm Aby." She said instead, pressing a hand to her chest. "I'm not afraid of you. I would love to talk to you, though."

The girl ate the rest of the fruit finally. It seemed as if she were testing if it were poisoned before she ate it. "I am Jomana."

"That's a beautiful name." This was her chance to learn more about this place and what was going on. "Jomana, why were you tested so young to see if you could have children?"

Jomana's brow furrowed in confusion at the question. "The man wanted me. He said I was the prettiest and was to be his first wife. When I did not have a child right away, he told Akar that I was broken. That I had been cursed and would spread it to others if I wasn't thrown away."

The mere thought was barbaric. She didn't even want to think about what it meant that Jomana would have been called the first wife. It seemed as if she thought of it as an honor.

"How have you survived out here all these years?"

She would have only been a child when she would have been left to fend for herself.

"The others they have thrown away took me in. They call us gods to strike fear into the others. If they don't behave and follow the mandates passed by the elders, they will also be thrown away."

Were there any gods, then? Or had the Elders made it all up as an excuse to use their power however they wanted?

"Are there any gods here, Jomana? Do you worship anyone?"

She shook her head, "Who would we worship that would give us such a life? Our only hope is to find places like this oasis before the Elders do so we have a chance to survive. We don't have a building in the sands to keep us cool. We constantly move for fear they will find us and kill us."

Had these men never heard of integrity? It was one thing to want to hold power over others, but this? They were abusing it. They were taking the innocence of so many and thought it was within their rights to do so.

"Aby?"

She heard Brandon call her name and dunked lower, trying to make herself as small as possible. "Go back into the brush where you were hiding. I'll get him away. They'll run if they see you and others coming. If you want to save whatever is left of this oasis for you and the others, you need to move quickly."

Jomana studied her curiously, tilting her head to the side as if it would help her get a better picture. "Why are you helping us? You're one of them."

She shook her head, "It's complicated. I'm not one of them. I'm not one of anything. To me, we should all be united and share the same wealth and happiness. No one should dictate to you what should be done with your body or your lives. Not to this extent."

Jomana offered her a soft smile before doing as she was told. It was only once she was sure that Jomana wouldn't be seen that Aby stood up. Brandon wasn't in sight, but that was for the best. It meant that she could put more space between him and Jomana. The least she could do was protect the girl when so many had failed to do so.

"There you are," she chirped as she approached Brandon. "Is my break over?"

He studied the foliage behind her before turning his gaze back to her, "Who were you talking to?"

She raised her brows at him before laughing, "I think the heat is getting to you. I wasn't talking to anyone."

He didn't believe her, but she hooked her arm through his so he wouldn't have a chance to go looking. It would hopefully give her new friend a chance to escape. If she followed through on her end, they would be leaving shortly.

"Don't we have more work to do? It looked like all the bladders were full, so I don't imagine there's more for us to do here." While she wanted to leave plenty for those exiled, she didn't want to give away that she knew.

He let her lead him back, occasionally looking down at her as if waiting for her to confess. If he thought it would be that easy, the version of her in this world wasn't very strong after all. Grabbing one of the empty bags from near their mounts, she flashed him a grin before heading to gather more.

Chapter Seven

It felt like it took hours for the warning call to ring out. The others around her all froze like deer in a headlight when it filled the air. All work ceased. Silence fell among them until they heard another call. This second call had everyone moving quickly. They stopped working, grabbed the bags or baskets they were filling, and ran towards their mounts.

Brandon had already mounted his when she exited, quickly tying her last bag to her mount. It took mere moments for all the bags to be secured and them to be airborne. Brandon kept close to her side, ensuring she made it far enough away that she wouldn't be harmed. It seemed as if being someone that hadn't given them children yet made her special. She still wasn't sure how she felt about it. Less so now that she had talked to Jomana.

The question was how she was going to be able to change anything about it. She doubted Amun Ra had brought her through to this world to change it. There was a lesson to be learned, though. Supposedly, it would be made evident to her. The only thing made apparent to her was the lack of integrity in the people that had power. From the sounds of it, this had been going on for a long time. One person, especially a woman, wasn't going to be able to change anything.

Glancing at Brandon as he led the final formation, she wondered if she couldn't get him to join in. He had been shafted by the system presented. It also meant that he would know people who might be willing to join their cause. The only problem would be getting him to agree and not tell anyone in charge of it. The last thing she needed was for everything to blow up in her face.

She had expected them all to need to help unload everything they had gathered. Instead, many workers rushed out to take care of their mounts and began to unload things.

"They'll take them to the kitchens. The water will be added to our stores, and any vegetation that can be planted will be." Brandon came to her side, watching as they worked quickly. "We're only meant to gather the material. There are others involved in the rest."

Purposely, she hung back as everyone else filtered into the tunnels. It would give her a chance to talk to Brandon alone. As foolish as it was, she wanted to broach the subject to him before she overthought and backed out.

"You know," she began, turning her gaze towards him. "I can't help but notice that none of the younger men have wives."

He furrowed a brow at her, tilting his head curiously, "Hasn't your father already talked to you about this?"

Thinking quickly, she replied, "No, he only covered the women's portion. We're expected to have two children for the man who is chosen for us. If we have more, that means we're blessed."

Silence reigned for a moment before he spoke softly, "It's different for men. We're supposed to be the ones protecting the women. We have to earn the right to have a family. Proving ourselves shows that we're blessed and means we'll have many children. It's why there isn't a limit on the number of women a man can have. Women can only have one man, though."

She barely stopped herself from scoffing at the mere thought. Wanting to make him think she was confiding in him, she chewed her lower lip.

"What if…. What if I can't have children, though?" she turned her gaze to him, allowing the fear she had felt before to show through. "What will happen to me?"

For a moment, she thought she had pushed too hard too quickly. He stared down at her, studying her closely. She forced herself to look away. The intent was for him to think she was ashamed to let him see her so weak.

He sighed, "I doubt you have anything to worry about. Your family has a history of being… fertile."

She felt disgusted by this conversation. Someone had just told her her family had a history of being fertile. How was that okay?

"And if I'm not? What if I'm cursed? As you said, everyone my age has already had their two, and I'm still waiting."

He chuckled, shaking his head, "It's because your father says you deserve to be a first wife. He wants you to be held above the others. Part of that is because of your family. It's not you, in this case. There hasn't been a male that has proven himself in a long while. There's no fresh blood for your father to give you to."

She could feel her rage at that sentence begin to boil. Years of pushing down her annoyance and anger served her at that moment. Letting the silence stretch between them a little longer, she raised the question.

"What does happen to women and men that aren't fertile? I'm assuming something does. Or do they become workers like those?"

He leaned back against the nearest wall, crossing his arms as he observed the work.

"Some of them do. Most, though? Honestly, most get sacrificed to the gods to appease them." He nodded his head towards the entrance they had come through. "Those things we ran from out there? They're the human servants of the gods. They're here to steal what is left of the world and make life harder for us. We also give the gods the children that are deformed. The Elders believe they'll have a better chance with the gods than here. And they're right."

She glanced towards him, studying his profile. "Wouldn't they be better here where we can protect them?"

He sighed, smirking at her, "Now you're getting into dangerous territory." Chuckling, he continued thoughtfully, "They wouldn't be better off here. This is a system where your appeal is in your looks if you're a woman and your strength if you're a man. They would also be given the least."

She turned her body towards him, genuinely curious. "You sound like you don't agree with it."

He froze, thinking over his words earnestly. She realized that he thought he might have said too much to the wrong person.

"I agree if you do. I think we need to do more for people. We're all in this together. At a point, the bloodlines will be too intertwined, and then we'll likely only be having children with deformities or mental issues. It would mean the end of our world."

She turned her gaze away, studying the people that were working so hard while they stood there. It was like a brush on her skin when his gaze turned towards her. This was the risk. She had told him that she disagreed with the way their system worked. Either he would agree with her, or it would end up poorly for her.

"Did you talk to someone out there?"

The question startled her enough to turn her gaze back to him with wide eyes. "Why would you ask me something like that?"

He shrugged, watching her closely. "Because I've never heard you voice such things until now. I know there was someone out there. I know you came across them and hid them. Did they plant these ideas in your head?"

And there it was. He might have disagreed with how this society ran, but not enough that he would stand on his own against them. She had gambled and lost. Time would tell what the consequences would be.

"What does it matter? I'm just a woman, after all. Soon enough, I'll be given away to a man and expected to give him only children." She tried to sound calm about it. In all honesty, she hated that she had given him power over her.

"It matters. The gods speak lies to try to dissuade us. You should know that."

Turning her gaze to him, she pushed herself from the wall, "I do. However, everything she told me, you just confirmed. We have a moral obligation to uphold. We aren't doing so. Instead, we cast people aside who we deem aren't of use to us. There are no gods in this land. There are only old men who deem themselves too important."

He grabbed her arm, yanking her back towards him. His face was twisted in anger.

"You would do well to remember your place. You can be broken and damaged so that no one will want you. Then you'll be nothing better than whoever you talked to today. You'll be thrown aside and left to fend for yourself."

She tugged violently against him, trying to break his hold, "Let me go."

He sneered before shoving her away, "Everything you have, you've been given by these old men you seem to condemn. You know nothing and are nothing."

She didn't bother to walk away calmly. There had been too many people witness to what had happened. Instead, she ran away, darting down halls without thought to where she was going. It was only a matter of time before he told Akar. There was no doubt that she would find herself either at the mercy of a man or thrown from the keep. Neither of which would help her learn her lesson.

She didn't know how long she had wandered the halls, but she didn't want to return to where the others would be. The further she walked, the more unused the tunnels seemed to become. There was an appeal in knowing she was walking where others hadn't. It was the same peace she had felt when walking through ancient tombs and temples.

Finding that peace meant more to her than anything. Finding a corner where she could see down each tunnel, she let herself take a seat on the floor. Drawing her knees to her chest, the silence that echoed around her brought her more comfort.

Amun Ra had said the lesson to be learned would be apparent rather quickly. It seemed, to her, that this all revolved around what was happening here. These Elders had been given the power and opportunity to help others and build a healthy society. Instead, they had used that power to benefit themselves. It also seemed that they only allowed other men to have proven themselves when it suited them.

What was the lesson here, though? The importance of morals? To have the integrity to stand up against all that was wrong with this place? If that was the case, she had already proven herself, hadn't she?

"Okay, Amun. I'm ready to go," she whispered to the silence around her.

Nothing happened. She sighed, leaning her head back against the cold stone. It would have been too easy if that was how she moved on.

Chapter Eight

She hadn't meant to fall asleep. One moment she was contemplating what lesson she needed to learn, and the next, she was being jolted awake by men roughly grabbing her. She hadn't heard them approaching, or she would have put more distance between them.

"What are you doing? Unhand me!"

"Akar says you're to be brought before the Elders."

Had Brandon snitched on her? Considering she hadn't let anyone know where she was and now was being presented to the Elders? The implication was there that he was to blame. She didn't bother voicing her concerns or asking to be let go. It was apparent they had no intention of releasing her until she was before the Elders.

Tunnels after tunnels went by as they carried her. They weren't necessarily rough, but they made sure they kept a firm hold on her. While she wanted to question why she was being taken, something told her that they wouldn't tell her. As expected, she was finally released, only to be shoved towards a large door.

"Go inside."

She didn't even bother to hide her glare. She aimed it at each of the men that had brought her here. They were all younger men, which likely meant they were also victims. The sound of the door opening before her ended the moment, though.

Inside was a large room lit by candles around the edges and a fire in the middle. There were no windows to the outside world, something she had expected from her time here. Sitting around the edge of the room, each with a candle to illuminate them, were the Elders she had heard so much about.

"You have been brought here as it has been decided that you are ready to be given to a man." One of the Elders spoke, his voice echoing around her.

She came to a halt before the fire, drawing strength from its warmth. The chill in the air made her think they were much further underground than she was used to. She didn't respond to the Elder, simply stared at each one in turn. They wanted power. They would have to be the ones to continue.

"However, it's been brought to our attention that you disagree with society rules. You've been outspoken and have even endangered yourself before gifting society with your future."

Again, she remained silent. This time she didn't bother to look at the Elders. She let her gaze drop into the fire and watch the flames dancing there.

"Do you deny that you have spoken out against us? We have been told that you wanted the sacrifices to stop. You want the deformed to be kept and protected, though they bring nothing to society. You want the Elders to have less power and give it back to the people. Do you deny this?"

She had planned to stay silent once more. The truth was that either way she spoke, she would be punished. Either she would be thrown to the wolves and forced to fend for herself or given to a man that she had no interest in.

"If you deny them, you'll become his first wife."

Those words whispered hoarsely had her raising her gaze to meet Brandon's. This was how he would prove his worth? Was that how they all proved their worth? By weeding out those that would stand against them? Did Brandon expect that she would remain silent? He had voiced his intention to stick to society's rules and manhandled her as if he had a right.

A slow smile curved her lips. Brandon seemed to take that as a positive sign and returned the smile.

"I don't deny it. I think you've let power go to your heads. You've lost all integrity. This is your way of being able to get any attractive woman you want, whether they want you or not." She turned her gaze to the nearest Elder, chuckling softly, "Is that what you wanted to hear?"

Brandon stepped forward, shaking his head, "You'd really choose exile over me?"

"You're just like them. Exile is better than a man who thinks my only worth is between my thighs. You speak as if you care about the people who were thrown away, but you don't. You think they deserved it." She turned towards the Elders angrily, "Which one of you took Jomana? She was a child! You threw her away, saying she was worthless because she couldn't give you a child."

One of them spoke, the echoes hiding his location, "She had had her first blood. She was a woman."

"She was a child! She didn't deserve to be raped and thrown away. You tried to break her, but she's strong. She recovered. These people you give to the gods? They're more human than any of you will ever be. So yes, I choose exile over this prison. I choose to stand with the people you've thrown away when you should have protected them. I choose to stand on my own." Turning back to Brandon, she glared, "Good luck trying to keep others at bay. Once they learn the truth, you'll lose more. And they will. The truth always comes out."

Silence fell over the chamber, aside from the snap of the fire in front of her. The Elders seemed to think that she would have simply bowed her head and given in. This was too important of an issue to simply stand down. They were in the wrong, and they knew it. If getting rid of her would make life easier for them, that was what they would do.

"You have made your choice. At dusk, you will be removed from the keep. You won't be allowed to gather any belongings. You won't be allowed to say goodbye to your friends or family. Your father will be informed that you have been sacrificed."

The door behind her opened once more. The same men that had escorted her here marched in with the intent to grab her.

"You can exile me, but I'm walking on my own." The men halted and looked to the Elders for guidance. She laughed, brushing passed them, "I'm no longer one of you. These old men don't rule me. Nor do any of you have a right to touch me. Now, who is going to lead me to the exit? I'm ready to be done with all of you."

She had no idea where the confidence or attitude came from, but it was an incredible feeling. She had stood up not only for herself but for the people they had thrown away. Maybe she hadn't learned her lesson yet. She might find herself in that desert once more without help. It didn't matter at that moment. They were asking her to betray her morals to live a comfortable life. Nothing was worth that.

One of the men led her through more tunnels. They didn't go to the entrance she had seen before. Instead, she was led to a less used entry. She barely suppressed a laugh at the knowledge that they didn't want her to be seen by others.

She wasn't immediately released, though. It took a while for the sun to nearly set. After all, they wanted to try to ensure she wouldn't survive. The joke was going to be on them.

"Did you really stand up to the Elders?"

The voice was a whisper to her right. The man standing guard on her couldn't be more than seventeen. He didn't meet her gaze directly but glanced at her and then away.

She smiled to herself. It seemed her parting words were beginning to prove correct. "I did. They shouldn't be allowed to decide who we end up with. They shouldn't be allowed absolute power when they do nothing more than stealing the glory."

He didn't ask any other questions, but she had planted the seed. What happened after she left these walls would be up to them. She had expected there to be a bit more fanfare with her exile. Instead, it was only the man that was standing guard that saw to her exit. He unlocked and opened the door for her with a secret smile.

"Good luck out there. Something tells me you won't need it."

She would have liked to take him with her. Someone like him deserved to have a life that gave him hope. This wasn't her world, though. It wasn't the world she would be choosing to return to either. Leaving the keep, she didn't look back. There was no regret here. It was strange to realize how much she wanted to save the people there. She didn't belong here, though. There was no temptation to stay here. There were no tears at this point in her departure.

She didn't know how long she had walked. The sun had drifted below the dunes, and darkness descended quickly. The only thing she could do was continue walking forward. A part of her kept thinking the sand would swallow her as she had been before.

"Well, that went quickly."

The voice seemed to be the trigger. One moment she was surrounded by darkness; the next, a flash of light had her once more in the Temple of Noor.

"Wait a minute. I thought I was only coming here at the very end?"

She turned to where Amun Ra leaned casually against the wall. He grinned at her, casually waving at her.

"I thought about it, but then you'd miss out on seeing all this. I am quite a snack, as you say these days." He pushed away from the wall, that same cocky grin in place. "Don't you want me to bring you back here before I send you on to the next location?"

It would give her a moment to catch her breath before she moved forward. It would also give her a chance to ask him what her lesson had been.

"You said that went quickly. What was the lesson?"

He raised a brow at her question, not replying. Realizing he wanted her to try to figure it out, she frowned thoughtfully.

"Is it because I stood up for what I believed in? Even though denying it and following along with the others would've been easier?"

He chuckled, tucking his hands into his pockets, "It's called having integrity. Admittedly, this situation may have made it easy for you to stick to your integrity. In life, there will be many opportunities to turn away from it. You saw the consequences of following the wrong path, though."

She nodded, "They were all so unhappy but pretending to be because it was what they were taught. I never want to lose myself like that."

She had begun to realize that these lessons and the way she learned them would stick with her. She would remember each time things fell apart and every time she felt she had let someone down.

"Will I remember them all?" He raised his gaze to hers, studying her closely. "Every lesson? Every world? Will I remember how many people it feels like I've let down?"

He smiled softly, but there was a sadness to it. "We always do. The ones we letdown are the ones that stick with us the most. Even a god can't erase that. However, when you choose what world you stay in, we can blur most of the others. You'll remember the lessons you've learned, but not necessarily who all was a letdown. Or worse, if anyone dies because of your actions."

Those last words were whispered. It was as if he didn't mean for her to hear them. Turning her gaze to him, she wondered if the consequences of their action or non-actions haunted them the way it did mortals. She could only imagine it would be worse when you had an eternity to remember everything.

Not wanting to get both of them down, she offered him a bright smile, "So, do I get to rest between these jumps? Or is this where I dive into the next experience?"

"Are you tired?"

She thought she would be. Maybe she was riding high on the adrenaline of standing up to someone. Either way, she shook her head cautiously.

"If you're tired, you should rest on your journey. I can't promise that you'll get sleep here. Besides, don't you want to get through your lessons quickly?"

She didn't have an answer for that. Getting through her lessons quickly meant she would be forced to choose what world she would return to. While this lesson and some others might be easy, there had to be something that would tempt her to stay in another world.

"Let's get this over with, all right?" It was better to leave some questions unanswered.

He chuckled, grinning broadly, "I like the way you think, Aby. On to the next world and lesson. When you're done, I'll see you back here."

It was a bit scary to think of being on her own in another world. She knew she could handle it, but she was used to someone being at her back. While the rules stated that Amun Ra wouldn't step in, she hoped that he would do so if her life were threatened.

Once again, the archway flashed before emitting a steady light. The theatrics were something she could do without, but she doubted she could convince Amun Ra of that. He seemed the theatrical type. Offering him a reassuring smile, she stepped through the archway once again.

<u>Chapter Nine</u>

When the light faded, finally, Aby blinked to look at where she was. This wasn't quite the opposite of what she had experienced before, but it had a lot more greenery than the Egyptian desert. There weren't any clues as to where she was, though. Searching the immediate vicinity, she was pleasantly surprised when she found the same bag she had been using. Her regular clothes weren't in it anymore, though.

The clothes in the bag were a bit different from what she had been given previously. It took her a few moments to understand what she was looking at. When she did, it gave her a good idea of where she was. The gown was from shoulder to ankle. It gathered at the shoulders in clasps and fell to her waist where it cinched. There was intricate embroidery along the edge of each piece of fabric. From her shoulders fell forward extra cloth that flowed freely in front and back.

If the outfit were anything to go off of, she would say that she was in a location heavily influenced by Rome. The downside of this was she hadn't done much research or studying on Rome since college. Even so, the outfit was beautiful. It made her feel feminine and strong.

Shoving those thoughts aside, she stuffed the extra clothes into the bag once more. She had a mission to complete and a lesson to learn. Neither of which would get done if she stood around admiring herself.

She didn't know which direction to take once again, but Amun Ra had dropped her off towards dusk once more. It didn't take long for her to see the lights from the nearest city, giving a soft illumination to the sky. She grasped her bag tightly, not sure who she would run into on the roads. Her hope was she would see Jazz, Baahir, or Brandon along the way.

It took her a few minutes to get through the greenery to where the road winded towards the city. There were still a decent amount of travelers going to town as well. To be surrounded by laughter and conversation made her feel like she belonged.

"Are you excited about the party tomorrow night? I heard it's to be exclusive. Only a few are invited."

It seemed that women were excited about the same things, no matter the location or time. Following the flow of traffic, Aby kept waiting for one of the familiar faces to pop up. Alas, she made it into the city without a single one. Was this part of her test?

She shoved thoughts of her lessons aside. She wanted to enjoy this experience. For a moment, she forgot that this wasn't just part of some bigger scheme. She felt like she was a part of this world. It wasn't necessarily friendly, but, in a way, it felt more real than the last world had. Merchants stood at booths lining the street, calling out to those walking by. Aby stopped at a few of the stalls, looking over the wares. She knew she wouldn't be buying anything, but it made her feel as if she belonged.

Reaching the end of the lane, she followed the women she had followed into the city. For some reason, it reassured her that she wouldn't get lost. Last time it had been Brandon that had kept her from getting lost.

"Do you plan on following us?"

She hadn't realized that she had been noticed. Glancing up, she met the gaze of the two women.

"I'm sorry. I didn't mean to. You just seemed to know your way around the city, and I didn't want to get lost." She offered them a shy smile, "I couldn't help but overhear about a party?"

They seemed to look her over, judging her clothes before one of them smiled at her. Amun Ra made sure her clothes said she was from money. She could certainly work with that. Even she knew some doors were just easier to open with money.

"I'm sure you could come. You look like you have the means to fit in. It should be starting in a couple of hours."

The woman beside her nodded emphatically, "It's quite a big deal. The wealthiest family is introducing their next child. It's her entrance into society."

Aby didn't think she cared about a debutante ball. Amun had said that she would get hints rather quickly on her path. If only for that reason, she should make an appearance.

"That sounds fascinating. I'll have to make an appearance later. You two have a great night, though." She would put a bookmark in that idea.

Stepping around the two women, she headed further into the city. People were shouting at each other from buildings on either side. It was what her experience when she had traveled to Italy had been like. Everyone seemed to know each other and were one big family.

"Are you going just to wander the streets? Or do you plan on making an appearance at your own party?"

She hadn't been expecting to run into Brandon, but lo and behold, there he was. He was glaring at her, his anger twisting his face into something unattractive.

"You know, if you want to find a woman, you really should try to smile more." She crossed the lane to him, offering him a bright smile. "You were saying something about a party?"

He shook his head at her, rolling his eyes, "You ran off, and I was sent to go find you. You know that everyone has been slaving away to get everything ready for you."

In this world, it seemed she was the debutante. She couldn't say she had ever had a party thrown in her honor. Even in her world, she hadn't even had a party thrown for her, including birthday parties. It was exciting on that alone.

"I guess we should get back if we're going to be ready in time."

He sighed, running a hand roughly through his hair, but he didn't argue. At least he seemed to have forgiven her at the moment. Brandon, once more, led the way. He took her down numerous streets, each street revealing more and more expensive homes. It seemed they were no longer in the shopping district.

Their final destination was the plot of land at the end of the last street. It was towards the center of the city. Considering the plot's size and the greenery she could see over the property's wall, it was an expensive location. She barely stopped herself from commenting on how wonderful this place looked. After all, it was supposed to be where she had lived her entire life.

Brandon walked into the house as if he owned the place. Aby wanted to give off that same energy, but she couldn't stop herself from looking around at everything. There were frescos on the floor and vases throughout. These relics would have made her weep if she had found them while on a dig.

"I brought her back!" Brandon yelled, disappearing further into the house.

"It's about time. I thought we were going to have to make some excuse. Maybe we could have faked an engagement."

Jazz stepped out, dressed extravagantly in a golden peplos. Her hair was arranged artfully. It was rather apparent that she was ready for the party that was to come. Baahir stepped out behind her, inclining his head to Brandon.

"Where did she run to?"

Brandon shrugged, not caring for the answer. "I didn't bother to ask. My job was to bring her back, and that's just what I did."

"I went to the hill outside of town near the main road. I wanted to watch the people coming to town."

Jazz grinned, "I think she was trying to see if she could pick a man before her party tonight."

Was that the point of this ball? To introduce her to society so she could be married off? She was starting to wonder if that wasn't the central theme behind Amun's locations. If so, she was going to have some words with him.

"Is that the only important thing about this ball? To find a husband?"

Jazz laughed, shaking her head, "We all know that we're what people want. They want to know where our money comes from. They think they can get to father through us."

Baahir nodded, "It works well for the men, but I would hate to be either of you."

That was accurate, though. Most men were able to sleep with whomever they wanted. Women tended to be under harsher constraints. She wasn't sure what the line of thinking was on that subject in ancient Italy, though. Recent theories presented seemed to imply that it was less of a taboo situation.

"I don't need to change, do I?"

She doubted she could ever compete with Jazz. This woman had such strong confidence she envied her. She wanted to ask her how she did it. What was the secret to having that take on the world attitude?

Then again, maybe she would. The point of all this was for her to learn lessons. Maybe learning how to gain confidence wasn't the lesson Amun had planned for her, but she could add her lessons into the mix.

"Let's get you ready for your big party," Jazz said, hooking her arm through hers to lead her out of the room.

She went willingly. It would make it simpler to ask her without the men breathing down their necks. She couldn't stand if Baahir and Brandon overheard. She wouldn't be able to live down the jokes and laughter.

The room she was led into was large, with doors opened onto the garden outside. She could have stayed in a place like that for her entire life. Laid out on the bed was another white peplos, but it also had a red cloth that would drape over her elegantly.

"How do you do it?" she asked softly, glancing up at Jazz. "You always seem like nothing can hurt you. Like you're the most confident person in the world. How do you do it?"

Jazz seemed taken aback by her question. "I don't really think about it, honestly." She paused, seemingly to consider her answer. "When I was your age, I was awkward. Father kept me locked away just the same as he did you. While I understand that most people want me because of the money that comes with a union to me, there was something about being wanted that helped me realize I had so much more to offer."

Had she felt awkward like Aby did? She couldn't believe it. Even so, it made her feel better. Maybe everyone felt like they didn't fit in and were always the second choice.

"Let's get ready for this party, right?"

Those seemed to be the magic words. Jazz moved quickly, helping Aby get into the outfit laid out for her. She had her sit near the open window, the breeze bringing in the scent of food cooking and the sound of laughter. This was another situation she hadn't had. Aby was an only child with busy parents. She would have wanted to have a bonding moment with a sister or even her mother. Jazz chattered on about anything she could think of while she arranged Aby's hair.

She could have fallen asleep if it weren't for the pending party in her honor.

"There we go. You're ready."

Jazz led her over to what was supposed to be a mirror. It suited the mirrors of the time. It gave her a distorted but near accurate look at herself. The woman staring back at her was not someone she had seen before. She was so used to wearing jeans and t-shirts. Dressed in a gown and her hair artfully arranged, it felt like she was a beauty queen.

"I look…. Amazing! Oh, thank you so much!"

She turned and hugged Jazz tightly, nearly bouncing with her excitement. Their laughter echoed off the walls around them.

"Of course, you look amazing! You always look amazing!"

Aby could only assume she meant her in this world always looked terrific. In her world, she barely cared whether she brushed her hair if it meant finding the artifact.

"You're just saying that." It was easier to deflect than overthink what Jazz was saying.

Jazz furrowed her brow before shaking her head. "No, I mean it. You always look so amazing. You don't care what others think of you. You'd rather bury your nose in a scroll than worry about the latest gossip. You're so smart, but you're always willing to help any of us, no matter how small the task. Sometimes I wish I were like you."

That single statement had Aby turning around on the seat to stare at the woman that was her sister here. "Are you being serious right now? You're what I want to be like. You're the life of the party, and everyone wants to know you. You know how to liven up any moment and make friends no matter the differences between you and others."

Jazz laughed, taking hold of Aby's hands. "I guess it's easier for us to see the good in others than to look at ourselves and reflect on what we have to offer. Don't let anyone sell you short. You deserve more credit than you give yourself. Maybe I'll practice trying to have a heart of gold like you."

Aby laughed softly, nodding. "Maybe I'll practice being the life of the party like you for once. Especially tonight."

"You sit tight. I'm going to make sure the guests are arriving. When it's time, I'll come back to get you, all right?" Jazz couldn't help the proud grin that spread across her face. This was the moment she had been waiting for. The moment her sister would be introduced to the world, and they could see just how amazing she was as well.

Aby didn't like the idea of sitting back here alone, but she didn't want to cause any issues. Offering Jazz a smile and a nod, she watched her walk out.

She couldn't help but spin, enjoying the feel of the fabric. While dresses hadn't been something she wanted before, she could see the appeal of them now. She still wasn't sure how she felt about the party that was being thrown in her honor, but she would fill the role.

It felt like hours when it had been mere minutes. Rather than sit inside the room twiddling her thumbs, she stepped out the large doors to the garden. She couldn't say she had thought about what Rome would look like in ancient times. She hadn't been to modern Rome in ages.

She could overhear the rumble of conversation nearby. There were music and laughter. For a moment, it left her feeling alone again. She had spent so much of her time on the outside looking in. While it wasn't the case here, old feelings tended to die hard.

Brushing a hand over the bushes near her as she wandered, she could almost imagine the dancing, twirling around the room with someone special. Aby had never been someone that thought they wanted to fall in love, but at that moment, she could believe in magic.

Ironic that she was traveling through worlds, and it was only now that she believed in magic. Maybe a part of her had always believed in the gods and what they stood for. For thousands of years, they had been worshipped and revered. It made sense that they would be real.

"Aby!" Brandon's voice rang out. "Don't tell me you ran away again."

She couldn't help but smile as she circled back to the doors. "No, I don't want to miss the party. I didn't want to sit in my rooms waiting either, though. Is it time?"

He nodded, holding his arm out to her once more. "It's time for the world to meet you. Just remember to stay on your guard. People always think that the newest debuted is the easiest mark." When she opened her mouth to protest, he silenced her, "I know you aren't. People mistake you being quiet as you being weak. That's not a bad thing."

She hadn't thought of it that way before. In a way, she had always felt lesser than others, like she had something to prove. Logically, she knew that stemmed from her childhood and wanting to gain her parent's approval and praise. It had never happened. She had pushed herself relentlessly to become someone they could be proud of and had still yet to garner their praise or notice.

Oh, she got the customary holiday card, but they never reached out to simply talk. They never asked how her day was going or if she was achieving her dreams. Hell, they had never even asked what her dreams were.

Shoving those thoughts away, she offered Brandon a smile as he led her towards the party. The music and laughter became louder before abruptly cutting off.

"Quiet, quiet!" It took mere moments for everyone to fall silent. Baahir was the one speaking, his voice filling the rooms with authority. "My father couldn't be here, but he has left me in charge, as expected. We're all here for an extraordinary reason. My sister has finally come of age. As is our family habit, we keep the younger siblings hidden until we're sure they're ready to be released on the world."

There was laughter throughout the room before Baahir continued, "My youngest sister is something else. You'll all see that soon enough. We're also protective of her. She is the youngest, after all. I expect you all to welcome her the same way you've welcomed the rest of us. May I present to you my sister, Luna."

Was her name Luna here? She could honestly say she didn't mind that at all. It hadn't occurred to her that she would have a different name here, just as it hadn't happened to her that the others would. If Brandon hadn't been holding onto her arm, she might not have stepped out. She had never been the center of attention before.

"Come on. You've got all of us to lean on. I know it can be scary, but you're strong."

Was this how siblings were? They always had each other's backs and presented words of encouragement? Offering him a smile and a nod, she let him lead her through the doorway.

Polite applause filled the room; every eye turned towards her.

Brandon leaned down, whispering, "Do you want to say anything?"

It seemed as if it were expected by how everyone was staring at her. In another world, she might have said no. She might have simply dunked her head and tried to disappear. She could tell that Brandon, Jazz, and Baahir held in her high regard, and she didn't want to let them down.

"Thank you all for coming. I know everyone has been curious about me. Here I am!" Soft chuckles rippled through the crowd, earning a smile from her. "I hope you all enjoy the night. Please, laugh, dance, drink, and eat. This isn't just a celebration about me. It's a celebration of us all coming together."

She could see the look of pride on both Baahir and Jazz's faces from the other side of the room.

<u>Chapter Ten</u>

Aby had never met more people in her life. It seemed everyone wanted to introduce themselves to her. At this point, she had lost track of all the names. If there were a quiz later, she would fail.

"I think you need this," Jazz held out a goblet of wine. "You've been doing an amazing job. I remember how tough my debut was."

Over the last couple of hours, Aby had learned the names of her siblings. Jazz was known as Calliope, Baahir was known as Quirinus, and Brandon was Avitus. She was sure she would slip and call them by the names of her world.

"Am I supposed to pick a husband from this party? Because I don't know that I want to be wed at this point."

Jazz laughed, throwing her head back. She had such a presence that something so small as a laugh could attract everyone's attention to her. She wanted to be that self-assured.

"Hardly. If that were the case, any of us would be married off by now. Baahir is the oldest. He should be working to have children and continue on the family name. Even he isn't rushing into it. We're young yet. I'm sure eventually that father will expect it. More than likely, it will end up with us all being married off within a year."

That nixed the idea that marriage had something to do with this world too.

"Do we ever see father?" Aby asked, thinking of her childhood and life back in her world.

The look of sadness that crossed Jazz's face seemed to answer it for her. Nothing was different here, either. She could only assume that something must have shown on her face because Jazz placed an arm around her shoulder.

"He would have been here if he could. He travels a lot because of the demands placed on him. We know he loves us. He ensures we have everything we could ever want."

Except for his love, Aby thought. Except for a hug that only a father could give to a child. It didn't matter. She hadn't had her father in her world, and she had turned out all right. It would be the same in this one.

"I'm fine. I think at this point, we would all find it strange if he were here."

Jazz gave her a look of sadness before turning back to the party. "We should dance. There's no reason for us to be down because of something beyond our control. Let's have fun."

She took the goblet from Aby's hand, placing both on a pedestal nearby. Before Aby could protest, she was dragged out amongst the people. Jazz led the way, moving smoothly to the music. It was all she could do to follow simply. Dancing hadn't been something she had done much of either.

In mere moments everyone around them was joining in. Even Baahir and Brandon made their way to the dance floor, finding women to dance with. She couldn't remember the last time she had laughed this hard. Her cheeks hurt from smiling.

A mere days ago, she would have said that her dream birthday would have been to have a warm, relaxing bubble bath with a documentary. At that moment, she realized she hadn't been living. Or at least not for herself. She had been doing everything to live up to some idea of what her parents wanted her to be. She had missed out on so much fun.

That changed tonight. She couldn't live her life for someone else. It would only leave her with regrets down the road. Breaking from the group, she made her way over to the wine and grabbed a fresh goblet. While she had occasionally drank before, it hadn't been this strong of wine. She found herself feeling relaxed and almost giddy.

"You look happy."

She turned, surprised to find an attractive man talking to her. His hair was a deep chestnut, curling like a cherub. That was about the only thing angelic about the man. He towered over her, a goblet of wine in his hand. Caramel orbs met hers, a brow raised as if in a challenge. His lips were full and quirked to match the look in his gaze.

"Why shouldn't I be? This is my party, after all. Are you having a good time?" It was ingrained in her to be polite.

He grinned, shaking his head at her, "You don't have to ask if I'm having a good time. This is your party, and that means you're the only one that matters here."

It didn't answer her question, which only made her more curious. "Shouldn't that mean you should also cater to my wishes and answer my question?"

She had never been so bold before. She wasn't sure if it was the wine or that these people didn't know the real her. After all, this wasn't her world. She could be whoever she wanted to be.

"Touche. You're right." He took a drink from his goblet before finally answering, "I'm enjoying my time. It's been a while since I've been to a debut. I thought they were out of date."

She shrugged, "I guess we just like to be memorable."

He chuckled, nodding towards the dance floor, "I suppose we should dance, then."

It wasn't even a question. Did he think she was desperate to dance with an attractive man?

Instead, she shook her head, offering him a polite smile, "Actually, I was just pausing for a drink before I went back to dancing with my family. Thank you for the offer, though. I'm sure you'll find someone more to your liking here."

She could just imagine how Jazz would take hearing that. Jazz thoroughly believed in living in the moment. A handsome stranger would be just the thing to fill her free time. Aby wasn't here to fall in love, though. Besides, while she knew some people were okay with something casual, she had never been that type of person. Every relationship she had had was long-term and had lasted years.

As she had expected, it didn't take long for him to find someone else to turn his attention to. She wasn't upset about it, though. She knew what she wanted and what she didn't. He would have been able to offer her a distraction for a night. She was looking for something that would last her a lifetime. Considering the mission she was on, she knew she could never offer someone else a lifetime in her given situation.

As she had said, she let herself be wrapped once more in the music and danced alongside Jazz. It felt as if a hole in her chest was being filled at that moment. The loneliness and wanting to feel like she had a family of her own was fulfilled at that moment. Maybe not entirely, but she could describe it as warmth settling in a hole she had felt for years.

There was a part of her that didn't want to return to her world. She didn't want to return to a place where no one reached out to her. She didn't want to celebrate another birthday or holiday alone. Every year was another wish that went unanswered. At this point, she wondered if her parents even realized they had a child.

She couldn't count how many hours they spent dancing and laughing. It wasn't until the sun began to brighten the sky that she realized they had partied the night away. Jazz leaned heavily on her, having drank more than she probably should have. Brandon and Baahir had disappeared some hours ago with the women they had gotten to dance with them.

It seemed as if everyone had had a great time. Her debut could be considered a success. While it probably seemed strange that it had been her debut and yet she was the one taking care of others, she wouldn't have it any other way. Helping Jazz down the hall towards her room, she couldn't help but laugh when Jazz mumbled something about wanting more sweets. It seemed she still had a sweet tooth here too.

It took mere moments to have Jazz tucked into her bed. While she didn't want to go to bed herself, she knew it had been days since she had gotten any sleep. Amun told her that she needed to sleep while she was on her missions. Considering everyone else was already in bed, she couldn't see a reason to avoid it.

Even as she said such, she found herself stepping out into the garden to watch the sunrise. There was a lot of work to do yet, but she wrapped herself in the peace she felt at that moment. It wouldn't last. It rarely ever did, but she had learned to take these moments of peace when they came.

Without the noise and the excitement, she finally felt the exhaustion sneaking up on her. She didn't bother fighting and found she was asleep as soon as she hit the bed.

When she woke hours later, it was the sound of laughter from the hall that pulled her from the darkness. It felt as if she had had a long blink and nothing more. Pushing herself up, she paused to listen. It sounded like Baahir and Brandon were still entertaining the women from earlier. Maybe they were closer to being married than Jazz had implied?

She didn't bother changing out of the peplos that Jazz had set out for her last night. It was far too beautiful, only to be worn for a special occasion. Heading into the hall, she peeked in Jazz's room, only to find her still asleep. The only part of her body that could be seen was her hand from under the blanket.

"Luna!" Brandon called down the hall. "I know you're the one awake. Get Callopie up. We can't let her sleep the entire day away."

Baahir laughed, "Only if we were to have another party tonight."

That was not something Aby wanted to endure again. She hadn't realized how exhausting it was to party through the night. She had spent so many years working on dig sites she had missed the party years.

Entering Jazz's room, she shook her arm, ignoring the groans of not wanting to get up that poured forth. That was something she was used to as well. She pulled the blanket back, exposing Jazz to the cooler air. Knowing that she could just pull the blankets back up if she wanted, she tossed them across the room to the floor. Covering back up would mean getting out of bed. That should be enough to get Jazz up for good.

"That's just evil," Jazz murmured, groaning as she tried to roll over for warmth. They both knew it was useless.

"Brandon and Baahir said not to let you sleep the day away because we aren't having another party tonight."

That worked well for Aby, though. She wanted to spend her day exploring the city. Staying within these walls wouldn't likely show her what her lessons were. For some reason, she felt strangely optimistic about everything at that moment. Even though she was in a world she didn't belong in, she felt as if everything she could ever want was a possibility.

If she chose to return to her world, she knew she wanted to make some changes. Maybe it was time for her to set down her roots. She couldn't expect everything to fall into place, but most of the time, when she went on a dig, she didn't have a set place to return to. She could fit all her possession into a couple of bags. It made it easier when she jumped from a dig site to a dig site.

Baahir and Brandon were where she thought they would be. Both lounged on chaise lounge chairs with the women from last night resting against them casually. They both barely spared her a look before turning their full attention back to the men. It must have been nice to have that kind of adoration.

"What are you up to, Little Moon?" Baahir asked, grinning playfully as he twirled a strand of hair from the woman before him.

"I thought I'd go explore some. Seems better than sitting around here all day."

Brandon and Baahir froze, exchanging glances before turning all their attention to her.

"Luna, you know the rules. You aren't allowed to leave. Father made it clear."

She frowned, trying not to pout, "But I went out yesterday."

Brandon cleared his throat, pushing the woman aside, "You escaped yesterday. It's why we were searching for you."

Baahir nodded, "It's why father built the garden as big as he did. It's where you and Jazz are to spend your time. You aren't to be exposed to the outside world. You'll be corrupted and exposed to much more than you want to be."

"There are some horrible people out there, Luna. They'll take advantage of you and not lose sleep over it."

Shock was a good description of how she felt at the back and forth. She was a prisoner in her own home. The longer she spent in this world, the more she wanted to move on to the next. It was beginning to feel as if she were living through the saying, 'The grass is always greener on the other side.' It wasn't greener at all. It was suffocating and confining.

"But you two can come and go as you please." It wasn't a question. It was a statement.

They offered her sympathetic looks. "It's safer for men to go out into the world than it is for women. We're less likely to be taken advantage of, and we can't have children. That makes you more precious."

She was the equivalent of a brode mare. Her lot in life for them was to stay pure until, she was sure, their father picked someone for her to wed that would be beneficial for the family. She hated this world more and more.

"Are we having this discussion again?" Jazz yawned as she walked into the room. "I thought we had settled this a week ago."

Baahir shrugged, leaning back now that Jazz was awake to handle Aby. "I thought we had too, but it seems Luna keeps thinking this will change if she pushes it more."

Jazz linked arms with Aby, smiling softly up at her. "Come on. Let's get some breakfast and take it to the garden. Trust me; you don't want to be around these two while they're with their companions."

Chapter Eleven

Jazz loaded down a tray with fresh fruits, cheeses, and bread. She motioned for Aby to grab a couple of goblets and the pitcher of wine before leading the way to the garden. Aby assumed they would take a seat at a table of some sort, but Jazz led her to a gazebo-like building. There was a low table between two chaise lounges that mirrored the ones inside.

"It's better we spend our time out here. Brandon and Baahir tend to take over the house when they have companions over. It's never fun to listen to them brag about supposed adventures they didn't take."

She didn't want to agree, but she also didn't want to spend more time inside. If it were a choice between being subjected to more sexist talk inside or enjoying the open air outside, she'd pick staying in the garden.

Aby was pleasantly surprised by how easily she lost herself in conversation with Jazz. They lounged on their respective chaise lounges munching on the snack they brought out with them and sipping wine. She could imagine this would be how vacation would feel like. There wasn't anything immediately she had to worry about.

The weather continued to be excellent—the sun shined down on them. There was a gentle breeze that would rustle the trees around them every few minutes and offer them a respite from the heat. Jazz seemed to love to regale her with stories of Brandon and Baahir. She didn't care that it seemed as if Aby had forgotten her entire life.

There was an appeal to having this be how she spent her day for a couple of days, but this would have been tedious if it were her day-to-day life. There was no adventure or challenge. It left her feeling like her life revolved around being appealing to the outside world and yet protected from it as well.

"Don't you ever want to see more than this garden?" Aby interrupted.

Jazz paused thoughtfully before shrugging, "I guess I'm just used to it. When father is around, he'll take us out into town. It's just safer this way. Besides, who doesn't like to be pampered? When we marry, we won't be able to have such an easy life anymore. We'll be expected to provide heirs and ensure the household is running smoothly."

Aby had never heard of something less appealing than Jazz's concept of marriage. While she hadn't thought about the idea of getting married herself, she had always imagined it would be a partnership. She wanted to marry someone that she could rely on; who knew she was there for them as well. It made sense that they would be her best friend and want to take adventures to see the world she hadn't seen yet. She wanted to be a part of their dreams and journey.

She didn't want to be relegated to a piece of furniture that was used. The women that were keeping Baahir and Brandon company had seemed like articles of clothing to them. They simply lounged against them, making them look good while the men talked around them. Where was the companionship?

"Is that what you want?"

Jazz shrugged, "It is what it is. We don't have much choice in the matter."

She told herself not to push. Jazz seemed happy enough in her decision. Aby just couldn't understand it, though. The Jazz she knew had always wanted something more than this life.

"Are you okay with it, though?" When Jazz looked at her, she offered her a smile. "It's just us here. You can be honest."

She looked hesitant before answering, "Of course, I would like a chance to see what's out there and do more than just lounge around. I just know it isn't going to happen, so I don't let myself think about it much."

While it made sense, a part of Aby wondered if that wasn't why things were the way they were. If everyone was complacent in how things were, nothing was bound to change. She knew that the point was that these worlds were based on ancient cultures that would eventually evolve. It felt strange to be stuck in the less evolved version.

Aby let the conversation drop. Once more, Jazz took the lead and rambled on about anything that came to mind. This continued until the sun's last rays fell behind the horizon. Only when one of the servants came out to light the torches around the garden Jazz rose from her lounge.

"Come on. Dinner should be ready soon. Brandon and Baahir will be waiting for us. Hopefully, their friends have left for the day."

"They aren't going to be here," Baahir said as soon as she walked into the room.

For a moment, Aby wasn't sure who they were talking about until he held a letter out towards her. Taking it cautiously, she stared at the script she couldn't read. Before she could fake that she could read it, Baahir spoke.

"They send their usual apologies and hope you had a wonderful time at your debut, but business kept them away." He shrugged it off as if it were nothing. "You know how they are."

Jazz offered her a smile, holding the goblet of wine up for her, "You should have a drink. This is how it always is. Our parents are never at home. They expect us to run things here and make sure the house still stands for the far off occasion they do return."

She didn't want to seem like she didn't remember anything, but it also seemed likely that they wouldn't question it. After all, their parents hadn't been home in long enough that they were used to it.

"When was the last time they came home? I honestly don't remember," she said, taking the goblet from Jazz before flopping into the seat beside her.

Baahir thought about it a moment before answering. "I think it was roughly ten years ago. It was when Brandon had a girl he thought he wanted to marry. They wanted to meet her and make sure she was worthy of becoming a part of the family."

Brandon grinned, taking a deep drink of his wine, "Obviously, she didn't pass the test. Otherwise, I would be married with who only knows how many kids."

It was a hard thing to picture. Even Brandon from her world didn't seem the type to be ready to settle down. Aby had figured Jazz would be the first of them to settle down.

The fact was she wasn't surprised by this revelation. It hadn't been any different for her before this. At the same time, it hurt. She doubted that it would ever not hurt. The difference was that in her world, she had stayed busy. Every holiday or birthday, she would throw herself into her work. It was ironic that she was emulating her parent's livelihoods while hating that fact about them.

Dinner continued without a problem. Baahir and Brandon had other plans that they were anxious to get to. Aby had no doubt it meant another party or meant more time with the women from earlier. She knew her goals, though. With Brandon and Baahir gone, Jazz had every intention of going back to bed. If Aby had been able to escape here before, she could do it again. She needed to do it again tonight.

"Pathetic," she said harshly, crossing her arms as she glowered from the hilltop she had arrived on.

Even in a world where it shouldn't have mattered, she found the actions of her false parents hurt. It echoed the reality she knew all too well. When she had gotten up from sleeping, she had assumed it would continue to be a carefree day. She had wanted to go out and explore, but Baahir had reminded her of the rules. She still wasn't allowed to go out unescorted. Supposedly their parents believed someone would try to use one of the women to get into the family.

She had been willing to accept that. When the letter had arrived as they sat to eat dinner, it had brought back all of the memories of missed celebrations. The message had been short and simple. They were sorry they had missed her debut and hoped she had had a good time.

"Why did you send me here?" She yelled up at the sky, feeling as if her heart were being torn from her chest. "Didn't I deal with this enough in my world? Did you think I deserved to be reminded that I'm not good enough?" She kicked the nearest rock to her, cursing Amun for putting her in this situation.

"That's not very nice, you know. I could take offense to being called a bastard."

She jumped at the sound of his voice. He seemed to have a fascination with scaring her by appearing like that.

"What are you doing here? I thought you said I was on my own no matter what." She hadn't expected him to show up just because she had cursed his name.

He shrugged, strolling around her to inspect the foliage. "Yes, but, you see, I'm a god. I'm allowed to change my mind. And honestly?" He grinned at her, "I was bored. I thought I would check in just in time to hear you cursing me. So what have I done to offend you now?"

She wasn't sure she wanted to open that can of worms with a god, but she also didn't have anyone else to turn to. That thought alone proved how complicated her life had gotten.

"Why did you send me here? You knew what the situation was. If I needed to deal with that, you could have left me in my world."

He tilted his head curiously, "What situation are we talking about?"

For some reason, that question made her angry. He had sent her here and hadn't bothered to keep track of what lessons she needed to learn?

"What situation?" She said it slowly, enunciating each word. "The situation where it gets reaffirmed that I'm not good enough. My parents in my world had nothing to do with me, and this world is the same. I'm just tossed aside and forgotten. They couldn't even bother to come home for a big event. Just sent a letter saying they were sorry."

She turned towards him with a growl, "Do you think I needed to be reminded of this? My parents left shortly after I could talk! They threw me away and passed me from nanny to nanny! They drilled into me just how not good enough I am! I get it!"

She hadn't meant to start yelling at him. He was a god, after all. It was probably asking for death, but she had bottled this up for so long. It seemed natural to lash out.

"You were just a child! You can't hold their shortcomings against yourself!"

She laughed, the sound bitter and filled with sadness. "You're right. I was a child. I needed to feel like someone wanted me. I needed to feel like someone loved me. Instead, I was thrown to the side like I was nothing. They still don't give a damn about what happens to me." Remembering that this wasn't her reality, she grasped at the things that were the same. "Where were they for my birthday? Where were they for the holidays? For my graduation? Where were they for my first heartbreak? For the first time that I broke a bone?"

How many times had she stayed up in her world waiting for her parents to come home only to find out the next morning they had canceled? How many birthdays did she get a card and a gift one of her nannies had bought and signed for her? She wouldn't even know what they sounded like if it weren't for interviews.

"I've spent my entire life trying to be something they can be proud of. Hell, I'll settle for someone anyone could be proud of. It feels like I'm screaming, and no one's there to listen or care. I just wanted to feel like I was good enough even to be their daughter."

There was something cathartic in giving voice to the feelings that she had hidden away for so long. Feelings of not being good enough, feelings of shortcomings, feelings of being worthless. It felt as if the world were resting on her shoulders at that moment, weighing her down. Crumbling to her knees, she buried her face in her hands, sobbing violently.

What had she ever done to deserve this life? What gods had she angered to be tortured like this? She hadn't expected him to interact with her. He was only here, as he had said, because he was bored. Much to her shock, though, Amun knelt before her, placing a hand on her shoulder in comfort.

"You did nothing wrong. You're holding the sins and burdens of others on your shoulders. You can't live your life waiting for someone to approve of you. You have to live your life for yourself. Chase your dreams." His following sentence was mumbled under his breath, "Perhaps this is what's been holding you back from your true potential."

She looked up at him then, tears still streaming down her face, "Am I that unlovable? Everyone that has ever been with me found someone else either while with me or just days after they left. Hell, everyone always leaves."

It wasn't her intention to garner his pity, but that was what she saw in his eyes at that moment. Shoving his hand away, she felt rage rise in her.

"I don't need your pity. I don't need anyone's pity." She wanted to add that she didn't need anyone, but she was tired of independently holding everything together.

He chuckled, the sound strangely threatening, "I'm lowering yourself to offer you comfort, and you shove me away? You're telling me these things because you trust me. You think I have all the answers, and I do. You want the answers? Or do you want just wallow in self-pity?"

She opened her mouth to apologize only for him to cut her off, "You aren't unlovable. It's quite the opposite. People meet you and realize they aren't good enough. They aren't going to rise to your level. It's easier to date someone that isn't going to encourage them to be their best than to risk trying and failing. It's easier to settle than to push to become the best person they can be. You challenge people to challenge themselves. That scares people. Most aren't like you and willing to push themselves. They aren't ready to pull themselves back up when they fail and not take it to heart. So stop shouldering everyone else's failures onto yourself. Start realizing who the fuck you are."

She had never even thought that that could have been the answer. She was shell-shocked and could only gap at him.

"Go get some sleep. You're exhausted. And think about what I said."

Did he think she would be able to sleep after a god had told her how amazing she was? No one had ever been that candid with her. She knew there was a part of her that believed what he was saying because of who he was. It also felt right, though.

Chapter Twelve

Aby screamed as the house shook again. She struggled out of bed, glad she had fallen asleep in her peplos. The cries of others echoed around her, filtering in from the streets outside. Stone broke away from the walls and ceiling around her, crumbling to the floor. What was going on?

"Luna! Run! Get as far away as you can!"

Baahir's voice rang out down the hallway, the sound of yelling and violence filling the small space. While there was a part of her who wanted to help the people who had become her family, she knew he wouldn't tell her to run if it weren't necessary. Grabbing up the peplos, she ran out the back door into the garden.

The sound of fighting was even louder out here now that the stone wasn't insulating her from it. Had Amun Ra put her down in the middle of a war zone? Was he crazy? He had made sure she understood that he wouldn't step in even if her life were in danger. Not unless she had learned the lessons that he had set out for her. The night before had been an accident. She had technically called him. Honestly, she still wasn't sure why he would have answers besides explaining that he was bored.

She raced through the trees, running away from the house towards the back wall. Jazz had shown her an exit there that would give her a chance to escape.

"There she is!"

She gasped, glancing back to see three men racing after her. They were armed with spears and swords. They held them in their hands as they chased her. She did not doubt that they meant to cause her harm. Had they hurt the others as well? She kept trying to put more distance between them, but they had longer legs. Just as she reached the door in the back wall, she felt someone grab her by the hair and throw her back on the ground.

The air was knocked from her lungs as she struggled to get away from them. Their laughter rang in her ears.

"Looks like you're cursed. You should have asked the gods to be born to another family."

She tried to call out for Amun, but it was all she could do to not blackout with the air knocked from her lungs. After all this time, this was how she was going to go. She would never get to see what other lessons were meant to be learned.

One of the men nudged the other, leering at her, "Why don't we have some fun with her first?"

The man in charge rolled his eyes, "I don't think you want to touch this one. Gods only know where she's been at this point. This blood is tainted. You don't want their curse to follow you."

She didn't want to feel relief, but if she were going to die, at least it would be with dignity. Even as she accepted the idea, she couldn't stop herself from trying to scramble away. If anything, it seemed to entertain the other men. They jeered and laughed as they slowly followed her.

"Amun," she croaked, knowing she didn't have much time left. "Please don't let this be the end."

"Sounds like she's begging for her lover to save her." The man in charge of them leaned forward, grinning down at her, "No one's going to save you. You can thank your father for that. I'm sure you're siblings are already dead by now."

Her eyes watered at the thought of the other three being dead. This world had given her a gift, and now it was stealing her away. She knew Amun said she wasn't cursed, but it certainly felt so at that moment.

"Excuse me; I believe that one's mine."

The sheer joy and surprise she felt when she heard his voice echo around her was like nothing she could explain. This was the second time he had come to her. He had broken the rule twice and less than 24 hours because she needed him.

"Who the hell are you?"

Amun grinned, dressed as he usually was in a name-brand suit. He didn't look like he belonged here at all.

"I'm here to pick up this one. You see, she's currently on a mission for me. I would hate for all my hard work to go down the drain because you got sword happy. Now, if you'll excuse us."

"Don't think for a moment you can take our prize!"

One of the other men raised his blade and made it to attack Amun. With a flick of his wrist, he sent the man flying before holding out his hand to Aby.

"I think it's time we got out of here."

She nodded, not trying to talk. Placing her hand in his, she could only stare up at him in awe. He had actually come to her rescue.

She had become used to the flash of light the accompanied being transported back to the Temple. It didn't leave her disoriented at this point. Even so, Amun simply released her before shaking his head.

"You're quite a lot of trouble these days. I thought this would be easier. Do you just attract trouble?" Voicing the question had his brow furrowing thoughtfully. "Maybe it isn't you that's attracting the trouble, per se. Maybe Osiris figured out that I was involved. He would love to stir up trouble along the way."

The idea seemed to please Amun. Perhaps this was all a game to the gods. They tried to get in the way of each other and enjoyed every moment of it. She didn't like the fact that her life hung in the balance because of it.

"Either way, I'm sure you got the gist of what your lessons were for this world, right? Otherwise, I have to send you to another world with the same lessons. I don't think either of us would enjoy that."

She thought about it for a moment. There hadn't been anything that had stood out for her directly. Could it have been something about appreciating what you had? That didn't seem right. It didn't seem like a lesson that would improve how she dealt with the world or herself. Remembering what he had said that night on the hilltop, she tilted her head thoughtfully. Forgiving herself for the past was part of it.

He had mentioned lessons, though. That was plural and implied there was at least a second one. She could feel Amun watching her, waiting for an answer. While that would have usually made her want to provide a solution more quickly, she wanted to make sure it was the correct answer. Instead, she thought back over everything that had happened. If anything, she felt like the purpose had been for her to see just how strong she was. Even the reminders of her past had felt like they were meant to show her how strong she had been.

"I think you meant for me to learn forgiveness and just how strong I am. Like I've been through a lot. Regardless of that fact, I've pushed through. I've never taken failure as an option. It was always a small setback that allowed me to reassess my plans."

He grinned, shrugging, "Close enough. It's normally called self-worth, but I'll take that as a good explanation of it. It looks like we can keep moving forward."

"Not quite."

Another voice filled the space between them, earning a curse from Amun. Amun looked annoyed by the interruption.

"Do we really need to do that? Why don't I send her on to her next task, and then we can talk?"

The flash used to see when she was transported to a new location filled the Temple once more. This time it revealed a tall, gorgeous woman. Aby did not doubt that she was the most beautiful woman she had ever seen. Her hair looked like black silk as it spilled down her back. She was dressed as if she had stepped out of ancient Egypt before appearing here. Deep emerald green orbs met Aby's for a moment before focusing on Amun.

"I think we talk now before you torture this child anymore. Both you and Osiris have some explaining to do. Set her up someplace more comfortable than this forgotten place and come to the chamber. Depending on what happens there, will decide whether she travels on or not."

She didn't say a word to Aby as she disappeared in that flash of light once more. For a moment, the silence stretched between them. Amun sighed, shaking his head in annoyance.

"Looks like you get a reprieve."

Aby didn't bother to hide her curiosity. "Who was that? She's gorgeous."

He gave her a bland look as if her words were ridiculous. "Yeah, Primordial gods tend to be attractive. Then again, so do gods, in general. That was Naunet. She represents the abyss of the Underworld. When she says you're meeting with the other Primordial gods, you shut up and do what you're told."

"I guess that means you have to go, then." She clutched her hands together before her, rocking back onto her heels and forward once more.

He nodded, "I do, but I won't leave you here. She's right. This is a forgotten place. I'll take you back to my place. You can get some sleep or whatever until I can return and send you on to the next location."

She was going to his place? Did he mean his temple? Or was this where he lived in the modern world? For some reason, that made her more nervous than all of the other worlds she had traveled to.

"It shouldn't take long. They'll likely give Osiris and me a speech about our responsibilities as gods, and then we can continue what we were doing." He offered her a grin, "You ready to see where a god lives?"

Trying to hide her nerves, she grinned back, "I'm assuming a penthouse apartment?"

His smile faltered as if she had stolen the surprise away from him, "Well, you didn't have to spoil it."

There was another flash of light as Amun transported them to his penthouse in New York City. Aby had never had a problem with heights until that moment. Even glancing out the windows at the world below made her stomach pitch.

"So this is how a god lives?" she tried to joke, but Amun simply shrugged it off.

"If you want something to eat, there's plenty of stuff in the fridge. Even gods enjoy eating good food. Otherwise, make yourself comfortable. I'll be back to send you on."

Those were his parting words as he disappeared. With him gone, she felt like she could breathe a sigh of relief. His apartment was as she expected once he confirmed he lived in a penthouse. The space was large and open. A sectional couch faced a fireplace with a painting of Egypt hanging above it. The living room, dining room, and kitchen were all open to each other. They had the same color scheme of dark material and stainless steel. The table was a rough slab of wood that would sit eight people.

Wandering into the kitchen, she could admit that she was curious what a god would keep stocked. Opening the fridge and freezer, she was pleasantly surprised. It looked like Amun was secretly a bar fiend. His fridge was filled with beer, condiments, and take-out boxes. The freezer was stocked with bar food you could toss in the oven. It had the staples of mozzarella sticks, wings, potato skins, and jalapeno poppers.

She could just imagine his apartment would be fantastic for Superbowl. Heading back to the living room, she let herself flop onto the couch. The expectation was that it wouldn't be a comfortable couch. A part of her doubted that he would be the type of person to lounge on a sofa at downtimes. While he told her to make herself at home, she didn't see herself wandering to see what else was hidden in his domain.

The couch was quite comfortable. She wasn't sure if it was because it came from money or if Amun had put thought into it before he bought it. It was another moment when it felt like it was a long blind, and suddenly Amun was waking her up.

"I'm glad to see my couch meets with mortal approval."

She sat up with a yawn, glancing around before feeling her cheeks heat at the fact that she had fallen asleep again. Honestly, though, she hadn't felt this safe when she was traveling. She knew no one would come for her while she was in Amun's apartment. It just felt right.

"How did the meeting go?"

He shrugged, brushing it off, "It was as I expected. We were given a talk. Naunet told me to make sure you're fed and then to finish the lessons. They don't believe in halting a task partway through."

A part of her had hoped Naunet would halt everything. That same part had hoped that it would mean she would be stuck among the gods instead of sent back into the world she knew.

"I'm sure you've seen what I have. Is there anything you want to eat? Otherwise, we can order something."

She offered him a forced grin, feeling strange at his question. "We can eat whatever."

He nodded, "I'll order some pizza. Naunet said no football food. You can eat a few slices, and we'll send you on."

Aby wasn't sure how to handle what she was feeling. The more time she was spending with Amun, the more she thought she could trust him. He seemed concerned for her welfare and wanted to make sure she was taken care of. Even his apartment felt like a safe place for her to be. Logically, she knew she could have felt safe here because Amun had something at stake to see her through.

It seemed foolish to bring it up. After all, he was a god. She was just a mortal. She didn't want to think about it. Luckily, Amun was more than happy to talk the entire time until the pizza arrived. He explained to her how things worked with the Primordial gods, that they used meetings to keep the others in check.

While she loved the education, her mind wasn't in it at that moment. The more she thought about it, the more she had to admit that she could be developing feelings for Amun. Perhaps that was one of the lessons she was meant to learn. Again, she hesitated on broaching the subject to him as he handed her slices of pizza.

The pizza was delicious. While she hadn't been hungry before, that first bite seemed to set her stomach growling, and she couldn't get enough. Each of the slices was larger than she was used to but delicious in each bite. She didn't even realize how many pieces she had eaten until they were gone.

Amun quickly cleaned up the mess, leaving her sitting in the living room without a thought. Considering her last lesson had been to learn her self-worth, she wouldn't allow herself to cower because she didn't want to confront him simply.

Getting up, she followed him into the kitchen.

"Is one of my lessons to learn to love?" she asked hesitantly.

She refused to meet his gaze, staring down at where her fingers tangled together. Perhaps she was foolish. There was no way that a god would dare to love a mortal like her. At the same time, he had broken his own rule multiple times. She also remembered what he had said about her that she challenged people to be better, to reach their potential.

He shrugged, "I would say yes. Learning to love is an important life lesson; to love yourself and to love others. I would be remiss if I didn't include it in your lessons."

It wasn't quite a confession, but he did agree. He wanted her to learn to love. Perhaps eternity was a long time to be alone. She couldn't fault him for wanting someone with him. He had said in the beginning that Osiris wanted her because of the potential she had. It was a reach, but it seemed so likely.

"I think I understand now," she said softly, forcing herself to look at him. "I think I could love you, Amun."

If she hadn't been looking, she might have missed the look of surprise that crossed his face. Had that not been what he wanted? Instantly she regretted having said anything.

"Aby," he started, turning his gaze to the windows that surrounded them. "I'm not meant for the type of love you want to give. You're giving it to the wrong person." He sighed, running a hand roughly through his hair. "You're still so sensitive. I don't know how to say this without undoing all the work you've done so far."

She knew where this was going. "You don't have to say anything else. I understand. I just thought maybe, but you broke your rule and said all those things."

Turning his gaze to her, he gave a sad smile. "I meant what I said when you questioned me that night. I was bored. There are some nights where there isn't anything to do, even as a god. Those things I said to you were the truth, though. I understand that this might have been confusing. You see me as your only security in the world right now. I should have thought of that and been more cautious. I'm sorry about that."

She shook her head quickly, feeling awkward for having brought any of this up. "It's not your fault. I'm not used to people telling me how highly they think of me. I promise this won't make things strange between us."

Chapter Thirteen

Splash!

To say she hadn't been expecting the sudden submersion into the water was an understatement. Every time she had been transported through the Gate of Noor, she had ended up in a sticky situation.

Chased by murder-enraged men? Check

Stranded in the middle of a desert? Check twice if she took into account how this all began.

Pushing herself up, she shoved her wet hair from her face with a sigh.

"At least this one doesn't seem so bad." As soon as she uttered the words, she wanted to take them back. Those words were as right as a curse.

Wiping the water from her face, she took in her surroundings. Night had fallen, but without the light pollution she was used to, she could see more stars than she had seen in her entire life. Tall grass surrounded the body of water she was in, likely a river judging by the current she kept feeling tug at her legs. The gods had decided to swap her clothes into some kind of skirt and peasant-like top for once.

"Wonderful. I get to look like a Disney version of a gypsy this time."

Shaking her head, she couldn't deny that this place was gorgeous. If there was ever a place that she could have imagined living when she wasn't digging up history, it was here. She meant that when she returned to her world. At this point, she had no intention of picking another world. It had already proven too complicated.

"Do you always make it a habit of dropping into a bath with a stranger?"

She froze, closing her eyes and taking in a deep breath. How had she missed that someone else was here? Turning slowly to the shadows cast by the grass, she could only barely make out the shape of a man reclining against a rock.

While every part of her wanted to run the other way, she knew that there was a lesson to be learned if she was brought here. Clearing her throat, she crossed her arms over her chest, trying to look as intimidating as she could, looking like a drowned rat.

"Do you always hide in the shadows watching a strange woman that appeared in your bath?"

Yup, she was undoubtedly proving herself to be an idiot. At least talking to men in any world didn't change. She never failed to embarrass herself.

The stranger chuckled, pushing forward in the water. He, at least, didn't stand up. She probably would have become a strawberry with how red her face turned. There wasn't much light from the moon to help, but something had her taking small steps backward to maintain the distance between them. Even with him kneeling or crouching in the water, there was something innately dangerous about him.

His hair was sleeked back from the water, his beard catching fine droplets. She knew nothing about beards, but his seemed well maintained. For a moment, she wondered what it would feel like. Quickly shoving that into the inappropriate box, she focused on the man that could very well be a problem. His eyes were light, looking almost silver in what little moonlight there was. Sunkissed skin appeared darker than her own at night, making the dark ink she could see peeking out from the water even more intriguing.

To sum it up, he was hot. That was the only thing she could say about the matter. She honestly couldn't think of a time she had seen someone that attractive. This could be a problem.

"Is this better?"

Not really, she thought. She would have preferred not coming face to face with a god when she looked like a drowned rat, but beggars couldn't be choosers.

"Sure, we'll go with that. So where am I exactly?"

He arched his brow in a way she had only ever seen the Rock do. Still just as hot. "I'm assuming the gods brought you here for a reason. It's not often you find someone appearing out of thin air. They don't seem to like you very much, I take it."

He had a point. It seemed as if she had become a cosmic joke and the gods just kept rubbing it in.

"Still doesn't answer any of my questions."

Once more, he flashed that killer grin at her. He had to be related to Amun or something. She had never met anyone that could look so carefree and attractive. It was an art form for the gods.

"You would be in the land of Eupara."

At this point, she wanted to slam her head into a solid object repeatedly if it would be of any help. He might have been attractive, but it didn't seem like intellect was also a trait.

This time he threw his head back with a laugh, startling her enough that she jumped and lost her footing. Once more, she found herself submerged only to be dragged back to her feet by the god before her.

"Careful, or you'll drown." Once he was sure she could stand on her own, he continued. "I understand that you don't know what Eupara is. And no, I'm not an idiot." He had an accent that she couldn't place. It made her want to continue listening regardless of what he had to say. She didn't trust it. "Eupara is what you see. Lush lands for farming, freshwater, and fish. It is as close to paradise as we have. As such, we have to protect it. Which makes your appearance a problem."

She blinked, taking a cautious step back. "Are you threatening me? Cause I'm not a threat. You could probably break me with one arm."

He pulled back as if she were insane. She could have been at this point.

"I don't think you're a threat. As I said, the gods brought you here for a reason. For that alone, you're protected. However, if I hadn't been here, you would have been at the mercy of the land, and it is unforgiving."

It made sense. She still didn't trust it or him. Not once had she appeared before someone when coming to a new world. It made it seem like Amun was up to something. Then again, he had mentioned that Osiris might try to get in the way. Was this one of those moments? Could this god of a man be someone Osiris had placed in her path to get in the way?

"You wouldn't happen to know Amun or Osiris, would you?"

She had no idea why she asked point-blank like that, but she was done with games considering what she had been through. She hoped her life lesson wasn't to be bold. That would quickly bite her back if she had to guess.

He furrowed his brow in thought, staring off beyond her right shoulder. She was tempted to turn and make sure there wasn't someone there watching.

"I don't know of anyone by those names. If they're people the gods told you to find, we can look for them. After we get out of the water, of course."

Did he think she wanted them to start looking for someone while he was naked? Then again, she had appeared out of nowhere in his bath. It wouldn't be too far of a stretch.

"Do you have a name?"

It was such an odd way of asking, but it was also nice to tell someone her real name.

"My friends call me Aby. What's yours?"

He inclined his head towards her as he made his introduction. "I'm Gunnar." He seemed hesitant about continuing. "While I will be more than happy to call you Aby in private, if you're to travel among people, you need a stronger name of Eupara. Would you mind if I gave you one that fits?"

She nodded, unsure if she was making the right move, but he did have a point. She wanted to fit in as best she could. What she hadn't been prepared for was how closely he regarded her while he came up with a name. Shouldn't it have been easy?

"Thurid. That is a name that fits you."

It was pleasantly surprising, but she wanted to know what it meant. While she usually would have looked it up through her phone, that wasn't an option in such a place.

"What does it mean?" He gave her a look of surprise as if he hadn't thought she would ask for more detail. As far as she knew, he could have decided to name her something derogatory. It was better she knew what she was being called. "I should know what my name means when people call me such."

Again, he inclined his head towards her, "Yes. You're right. It means Thunder. You appeared quickly and loudly. Like Thunder."

She supposed it could have been worse. At least her grand entrance had made an impression.

Offering him a slight smile but deciding it was better not to comment on the name, she motioned towards the shore. "Any chance we can get out of the water? I am soaked through and don't have a change of clothes with me."

He glanced down at her before grinning. "We might want to find you something else before you come into town with me. They'll already assume the worst with you sleeping in my home, but I don't need them to think you are a woman of the night."

It took her far longer than it should have to understand his meaning. It caused her to glance down at herself where the clothes clung to her like a second skin. There was nothing left to the imagination. She gasped, crossing her arms protectively.

He held up both hands to sign that he meant no harm before turning his back towards her. "If you'll follow me, I have something you can put on over your clothes to at least keep you warm until we get to my home."

"Please tell me that also includes clothes for you to wear."

His chuckle was the only answer she received. For a moment, she stood where she was, shivering in the water. She wanted to give him a chance to at least get something on before she followed. The last thing she needed was to be caught ogling another god. That had been embarrassing enough. Even now, she questioned whether she had confessed a crush to Amun. A crush on a god? Was she out of her mind?

The fact that he had handled it so quickly and smoothly made her believe that it was a regular occurrence for him. At least she could assume it would be forgotten before she saw him again.

"You can come out now."

Gunnar's voice had her gaze turning towards the horizon where he had tugged a pair of pants on if you wanted to call them that. They clung to him much like her own clothes clung to her. She wasn't going to talk about the fact that he was shirtless. Even from her place in the water, she could make out the scars that decorated his torso. Each one was a story. The part of her that loved history wanted to know what battles they had been from. Even though she didn't know the history of this world, curiosity was still there.

Heaven help me if they all look like this, she thought. Clambering through the water, she didn't dare meet his gaze. Because she wasn't looking, she jumped when he set a cloak about her shoulders. Once again, he raised his hands to show he wasn't a threat.

"Why do you do that?" Again, she hadn't meant to ask the question that had come to mind. Maybe the last couple of days were finally getting to her, and she had lost that filter.

"You're in a new place. You're skittish like a wild animal. I want to make sure that you know I'm not a threat so you won't lash out at me. You could be more dangerous than you look."

The thought of her being dangerous against a man like this was laughable.

She shook her head, offering him a friendly smile, "I'm hardly a threat to you."

His grin wasn't as carefree or open as it had been when he replied. "We'll see about that one, Aby. I think you're more dangerous than you realize." She wanted to question that but didn't want to risk alienating her only ally here. "Let's get you to my home where we can get those clothes properly dry."

Chapter Fourteen

The ride into town was a tad uncomfortable for Aby. Gunnar had her ride in front of him on his horse. He claimed it was to ensure she didn't fall off and that she could use his warmth. When the ride started, she had tried to stay as far from him as possible. It hadn't taken long for her to realize the wisdom of his words. Being soaked through with only a cloak to keep the chill of the wind from her skin was enough to have her leaning back against him.

He didn't mention it, but she felt the chuckle that rumbled in his chest. It was as close as he was going to get to know he was right. The town he took her into reminded her of something for an ancient Norse village. It was further downriver from where she had met Gunnar. He didn't go far into the town, but it was breathtaking from what she could see. Numerous longhouses stood near the center of town, with smaller buildings branching out to the village's edge. It looked like closer to the longhouses were building for trades. She could only assume the other small buildings were for individuals.

That was her assumption since Gunnar led them to one. He led his horse into a yard off his home, a shack built towards the back for housing the beast. Every structure was built with logs, almost like a log cabin. The roofs were made to look like the land around them with grass and other foliage atop it. She had never seen anything so unique.

He climbed down from the mount before reaching up to easily lift her off. She didn't even protest the handling as she pushed past him to touch the wall before her.

"This is beautiful. Did you build it?" She turned back to him with a glance, genuinely interested.

He nodded as he led his horse back to his shelter, "Aye. We all build what we want to live in and help with the community buildings. I wanted a place for myself and Vidar."

She followed after him, watching as he checked the horse's food and water, "Vidar? Is that the name of your wife?"

He acted as if she had hit him with how quickly he pulled back from his horse and stared at her. "Vidar is the name of my horse. I don't know of any woman that would want to be called Vidar either."

For some reason, his reaction had her laughing before she turned her attention entirely to Vidar. "I'm sorry Gunnar didn't introduce us properly til now."

She could almost pretend that Vidar bowed to her in return, but she knew it was likely her imagination. While she knew Gunnar meant for her to stay here with him, she felt too awkward to simply walk into his home. Instead, she occupied her time while he tended to Vidar by inspecting the outside. The logs were sealed together with some kind of mud. It was just another thing that made this house a part of the land around it. Behind the house, Gunnar had begun to plant his garden. She wasn't sure what he was growing, but she didn't have a green thumb. She wouldn't touch them unless he wanted them to die.

"I know it might not be much of what you're used to." Again he caught her off guard, walking up behind her. "It's cozier inside than it might look. I just have to get a fire going."

She laughed again, "Honestly, this is a huge upgrade from what I'm used to. I normally sleep in a tent in the middle of nowhere."

He regarded her as if she were strange before turning to head back to the front entrance. It was a peculiar concept not to have a lock on the door, but he also seemed to carry what he valued with him. She followed him silently, stepping into the darkened interior without a second thought. Technically, this was the type of thing girls were warned against doing in her world. She trusted Gunnar, though. Another peculiar concept to her.

Gunnar crossed through the home in the dark without a problem. It was like muscle memory of having lived in a place for a long while. Aby stood near the door, allowing what little light the night offered in. It seemed to take him no time at all to get a fire going. That was a skill she would have to get him to teach her. While she knew how to start a fire, she wasn't very good at getting it burning so quickly without lighter fluid.

It was only with the fire going that she shut the door behind her. Once again, she couldn't stop herself from looking at the house around her. It wasn't filled as she was used to home being. There was a simple dining room table made of wood with stools sitting around it. There was a makeshift wall that separated what looked to be his bed. It was a pile of furs on the floor, but it also allowed the fire's heat to reach it.

"There's a bathroom through this door." He motioned to the only other door in the house. "I know it's not much." Again with the protest of what he had to offer her. She wanted to reassure him that she didn't need much to be happy.

Rather than put her foot in her mouth, she offered him a shy smile, "About these wet clothes."

She barely kept herself from giggling over how uncomfortable he looked at that moment. It seemed as if he had forgotten about her predicament. It wasn't that bad now that she was inside with fire. Even so, he moved past her to where his bed was before returning with an oversized shirt that must have belonged to him. She stared at it for a moment before looking back up at him. Wasn't this the type of situation she had read about too many times in romance novels? She would wear his shirt, and it leads somewhere else. She certainly wasn't going to condone that.

"We can hang your clothes up at the fire so they'll dry faster, and you won't get sick."

Again, she looked from the shirt back up to him before sucking her lips in and releasing them. "If I wear this, it doesn't mean I'm going to sleep with you."

He looked genuinely concerned. "Is that how people are like where you come from?"

"I mean, it's not a given, but people tend to get the wrong idea when you wear their clothes."

He took a deep breath and cleared his throat, "This is just so your clothes can dry. If I were to take you to my bed, it wouldn't be because you're wearing my shirt."

She didn't know how to take that and didn't want to start analyzing it. As she had already proven with Amun, she was terrible at reading guys. Accepting the shirt from him, she offered him a shy smile once more.

"In that case, can you please turn away so I can change?"

He nodded, "I'll do you one better. I'm going to go to the longhouse and grab some food and ale. I'll be back in a bit. Feel free to get changed, and I'll return."

A part of her didn't like the idea of being alone in a new place, but he raised other valid needs. Food and drink before she got some sleep would be preferable. Something told her that Gunnar wouldn't let anything happen to her. After all, he knew she was brought here by the gods. That thought flared up her distrust that he wasn't there because of Osiris. Anyone could claim not to know someone.

She waited until the door closed behind him, listening to his footstep recede before she stripped out of her wet clothes. A part of her wanted to keep her underwear on, but even that was soaked through. It wouldn't be very comfortable. To be safe, she took the dagger she spotted on the edge of the table. She would make sure she was safe.

Laying her clothes out on the metal rod next to the fire, she made sure they were close enough to dry. She didn't need her clothes catching on fire. Tasks complete, she took a seat at the table once more. His shirt was large enough that it nearly reached her knees as if she were wearing a dress. It kept trying to slip from her shoulder, but she would deal with that struggle. Already it felt better to be out of the wet clothes.

It felt like an eternity for Gunnar to return. He rapped on the door with what sounded like his foot before pulling it open. She met his gaze from the table as he entered. He didn't speak as he crossed the room, setting a bag on the table as well as two horns and a bladder of ale. Once he secured the door, he returned to sit opposite her.

"I have some wild bird, bread, and some vegetables fresh from the gardens. I hope that will be enough for you."

He started laying out the food. He placed all of it closer to her as if he expected that she would eat it all.

Smiling, she shook her head, "I hope you intend to help with this. This could feed three of me. And I ate just before." She trailed off, not sure how to explain it.

"I'm glad the gods fed you before you came."

He had no qualms about digging into the food laid out before them. He held the bladder out to her, motioning for her to lift the horn so he could fill it. She held up both while she was at it. It almost broke her heart when a look of surprise crossed his face. Something told her he was used to taking care of others but not having anyone there.

"Can I ask you a personal question?"

He took a swig from the ale before nodding cautiously. She wasn't sure how to word this without it sounding invasive, so she simply asked.

"Why aren't you married? You seem to have a lot to offer, and you're used to taking care of others, but you're here alone."

He stared down at the meat before him, running his tongue over his teeth. She thought he wasn't going to answer. It would have been within his rights to do so. She was a stranger asking invasive questions.

"I was married once. She was killed, and I haven't found a reason to marry again."

Her heart broke at that moment. She had never loved someone enough to even date for more than a season. To love someone enough to marry them only to have them stolen away was unfair.

"I'm so sorry for your loss, Gunnar."

He shrugged it off, returning to his meal, "It was a long time ago. I'm used to being alone now."

She always claimed that she was used to being alone as well. It didn't make it easier. It just meant that you kept yourself busy enough not to let the loneliness creep in. It seemed they had that much in common.

She took a drink of her ale, pleasantly surprised by the flavor. In each world, she seemed to learn something new about her taste. It had her smiling fondly down at the liquid.

"What of you?" His question had her gaze raised to his. "Do you have a man back home waiting for you?"

Such a complicated question. Technically a man waiting for her was why she had run. She couldn't imagine returning to find Professor Sonstroem waiting for her. Romantically, though, there was no one she could even think of. That included past relationships.

"No, there's no one for me there."

He didn't question further, and, for that, she was thankful. They sat in companionable silence while he ate. Neither of them felt a need to talk. Occasionally she could fill his horn from the bladder, or he would offer to fill hers. After all of the excitement of the last few days, she appreciated the silence.

"Are you tired?"

The questions startled her as it broke the silence. Looking up, she realized he had finished eating and was cleaning up the remnants by putting them back in the bag.

She glanced towards his sleeping arrangements before grinning playfully at him, "See? I knew you would try to get me to sleep with you."

It took longer than it should have for him to understand that she was joking. When it finally occurred to him, he gave her that heartbreaking grin once more.

"I was planning on making a pallet for myself out by the fire and giving you the bit of privacy you could get." She knew he would be a perfect gentleman. "I just was curious if you were tired enough to sleep yet. If not, we can sit by the fire and get warm while your clothes finish drying. I'm sure that would be more comfortable to sleep in than my shirt."

She shrugged, quickly catching where it tried to slip off her shoulder, "This would be something that I would sleep in if I were back home anyway."

He leaned back, studying her closely, "What is it like where you come from? Aside from you sleeping in the middle of nowhere routinely."

She was sure that was confusing for him. "My world is the opposite of this one. Everything is complicated." She took a swig from her horn, trying to figure out how to explain it. "I spend my time in a tent in the middle of nowhere because I'm uncovering history. Some artifacts and relics are buried, and I uncover them." She lifted the horn with a grin, "Like this. We would lose our minds over finding something like this."

"Do you love it there?"

That was a trick question. "That's complicated too. It's what I've always known, but it's never felt like home. My parents don't care about me enough to be around. I spend all of my time traveling, so I don't end up feeling alone."

He nodded thoughtfully, "I can understand keeping yourself occupied, so you don't realize how alone you are."

She turned his gaze to him, "Do you do the same?"

He stared into the fire, lost in his thoughts, "I take on any missions that are needed to protect the village. The way I see it, I'm the most expendable one. I don't have a trade. The most use I am is for my weapons."

"Is that where all the scars you have came from?"

He grinned at her then, "You were looking, were you?" She could feel the heat in her cheeks as she blushed. "Yes, that's where they are from. I've spent most of my time taking on missions. When you fight alone, you tend to come away wounded more often than not."

She wanted to ask questions about his stories, about the battles he had seen and the missions he had completed. It was such a strong urge that she very nearly gave in. The only reason she didn't was that she was looking at him. She could see the bags under his eyes from lack of sleep. While she had rested recently, something told her it had been a while since he had gotten a good night's sleep.

"I would love to hear more about what you've done, but I'm getting tired. We should make up your pallet so we can both sleep."

It didn't take long after she brought it up. Gunnar took very little from the bed. Instead, he pulled furs from a chest in the corner she hadn't noticed. He spread them out on the floor before the fire, doing quick work before turning his gaze back to her.

"Did you want to change back into your clothes?" When she shook her head, he offered her a soft smile. "Go get into bed. Let me know if you need anything."

She didn't have to be told twice. Clambering under the furs, she was only momentarily taken off guard by the fact that it smelled like him before she felt sleep tug her under.

<u>Chapter Fifteen</u>

Morning came far more quickly than she realized. She could hear Gunnar moving about the cabin, though he tried to keep quiet. A part of her wanted to bury even further under the furs and ignore the world. She knew it wasn't possible, though. She needed to learn a lesson so she could continue on her way.

Groaning, she pushed the furs back and set up to meet Gunnar's gaze. He offered her a sheepish smile, holding up another bag that she could assume was food. This time she had every intention of eating the food provided.

"Morning," she yawned again, pushing herself up to cross out of the bedroom area to take another seat at the table. "You're up early."

He shrugged, "I don't tend to sleep much. I tried not to wake you."

"It's fine. I only just woke up anyway." When he held up the bladder, she stared at it for a moment. "Please tell me that's water. I don't think I could imagine drinking ale first thing in the morning."

He chuckled, "It's water. I'm not that much of a barbarian."

She took the bladder offered, drinking straight from it. It was much like drinking from a canteen. Once more, he spread out a plethora of food. There was meat, as there had been last night, but also fruits and vegetables once more. He again pulled out freshly baked bread that was still warm to the touch and cheese. He motioned towards the food, letting her take it first.

She grabbed some meat but mostly stuck to fruit, bread, and cheese. Breakfast was another silent affair. They both were focused on eating their food and not on filling the silence with conversation. It was only once they finished their food that both leaned back with a contented sigh.

"What do you have planned for today?" She asked, wanting to make a plan.

"Aren't we looking for your friends Osiris and Amun?"

She nearly choked on air at those words. For a moment, she had forgotten that she had even mentioned them to him. "We don't need to go looking for Amun or Osiris. I was trying to see if you reacted to their names."

He frowned, "Are you saying that you don't trust me?"

She raised a brow at his question. It wasn't anywhere near as impressive as his ever was. "Why would I trust a man I had just met? If you had been through what I had, you would assume everyone was out to ruin your mission."

Mentioning her mission only seemed to pique his interest. "What is your mission, exactly? What brings you to Eupara, and how can I help you complete it?"

That was the question, though, wasn't it? What was her mission for this world? She didn't have the slightest idea at this point. Amun had changed up how she appeared in worlds this time around. He had given her clothes automatically and had her appear in front of someone from this world. She didn't have to pretend to be someone other than herself.

"I honestly don't know. I'm supposed to figure it out as I go. There hasn't been much of a sign for what my mission is for this world."

He didn't press. For that, she was grateful. If she hadn't appeared before him, she doubted he would have believed her story otherwise.

"I have a few things to do around town. You're welcome to rest here, or you can come along."

As if she were going to stay tucked in a cabin instead of exploring this world. Every world she had been to before she had been locked away. She was going to see this one, no matter what it might cost her.

"I'll go with you. I want to see what it's like out there."

He gave her a curious look, but again, didn't question her. Instead, he started cleaning up the remnants of breakfast. "If you want to get dressed in your clothes, now would be a good chance. You're welcome to wear my cloak while we're out there if you're cold, though."

She couldn't wait to get back into her clothes. Grabbing them from where he had laid them on a stool, she hurried behind the mesh screen. It didn't give her complete privacy, but Gunnar had been a gentleman thus far. He had had more than a few opportunities to take advantage of her. Besides, she was used to getting dressed in less than ideal conditions.

Once more, she made quick work of getting into her clothes. His shirt was large enough to provide her with more than adequate cover. While she knew she should have given it back to him, she carefully laid it back on the furs to use for later. It was too comfortable not to sleep in again unless he needed it, of course.

"Are you ready to go?"

She popped back out with a bright smile, feeling more herself now that she was in her clothes. "Yup. Are we taking Vidar with us?"

He shook his head, "I'll let him out to graze in the yard, but he isn't needed for this. We're only going to gather some supplies and see if there is any indication to help you figure out your mission. I don't think you were dropped into this world before me if I weren't to help you."

His logic was sound, at least. Following him out of the house, she was once more enthralled by the village. People milled around talking, purchasing wares from the shops along the main stretch. Her appearance alongside Gunnar drew the attention of people nearby, though. The whispers started quickly enough.

"I'm sorry. I should have warned you that people would talk."

She offered him a reassuring smile. "I appreciate the concern, but I don't care what they think. I'm not here for them. You're supposed to help me, as you said. If they were supposed to be important to my mission, I would have been dropped in front of them."

It was slightly uncomfortable, but she shoved that thought away. Following Gunnar back to the paddock, she couldn't resist running her hand down his flank before a thought occurred to her.

"Wait, Gunnar. What are we going to tell them?" At his look of confusion, she continued. "They're likely to ask how we met and how I ended up sleeping in your home. I don't want to complicate your life any more than I already am. So what are we going to tell them?"

He hadn't thought of that either until that moment. He paused, watching Vidar as he contemplated it.

"We can claim that we met on my last mission. The man I hunted down had taken you, and I brought you here to ensure your safety until I can get you home. Does that work?"

While she didn't like the idea of being held hostage by a man, it wasn't far off from what had happened that led her to this place.

"It's better than what I could have come up with. I would've claimed something ridiculous as we had fallen in love."

She had meant it as a joke, but the look of shock on his face told her he hadn't even considered that route. That was embarrassing. Then again, she couldn't say she was surprised that romance hadn't occurred to him. Considering he was a god among men, she wasn't even close to his level.

As soon as that thought entered her brain, she shoved it away. Gunnar would have been lucky to have someone like her as his romantic interest. He wasn't unobtainable. As the saying went, though, old habits died hard. She would need to work on her thoughts.

He cleared his throat, shifting slightly, "I wouldn't want you to feel uncomfortable. I assumed if I had suggested something along those lines, it would have been inappropriate."

She couldn't stop herself from taking a step back to stare up at him as if he had lost his mind. Did he think she would have been offended?

"Let me make this clear. I would not encourage anything because I'm only here for a short time, but anyone would be lucky even to be your fake lover. You're a wonderfully caring man who has done nothing but put up with my imposition. You're an attractive man, and I'm surprised there aren't women fighting to warm your bed."

He had not been expecting that. For a moment, they stood in silence before both quickly looked away. Aby could feel her cheeks heating once more with a blush. She was usually never that bold. This entire experience was changing her, and she found she rather liked it.

"As long as I don't have to pretend to be super timid, I think we can make your plan work." She wanted to get back to their playful banter and not make him feel awkward. The last thing she wanted was for him to think she had ulterior motives.

He seemed to grab onto the topic change and offered a grin. "That shouldn't be an issue. It's rare for women to be timid, in my experience. Usually, that means that they were treated poorly for a more extended period than what you would have been exposed to."

It seemed he thought she was strong. She rather liked that thought. She reminded herself that he hadn't said such, though. It was a good chance that it was her imagination solely. Letting him take the lead, she was more than happy to follow along simply. People kept watching her without approaching them. It seemed like they were watching everything Gunnar and her did and how they interacted, waiting for a sign.

Gunnar spent most of his time stopping at the vendors to pick things up. It seemed normal for him to drop something off to be repaired or buy new items as a reward for the missions he had carried out for others. There was laughter amongst those around them. It felt as if she were on the outside of some shared joke. She couldn't imagine being that close to people that it was this easy.

"You have a look of longing on your face," Gunnar murmured, following her gaze. "Do you not have people you are close with where you are from?"

She shook her head sadly. "I thought I did. Just before I left, I was shown just how alone I was."

She didn't have to look at him to know he was studying her sadly. If there was one thing she hated, it was someone pitying her.

"I don't see you joining in with them."

He shrugged, watching them for a moment. "It's not because they haven't tried. I just never know if I'm going to come back alive. I would hate to leave someone heartbroken over me."

With those words spoken, he turned to continue through the village. As she watched more closely, she realized the people around them would call out his name or wave as he passed. Even if he felt like he was keeping himself removed, they still thought of him as part of their village. As such, they were all the more curious about who she was and why she had been brought here. She heard Gunnar telling a few of the shopkeepers the story they had come up with. Those looks of pity were easier to ignore.

They finally came to the center longhouse. It seemed rather obvious that this was the meeting house for most of the village. Even now, people were moving in and out of the building. Inside they were grouped in conversation. It was something so small, but, again, it made her feel like an outsider.

"You can stay here if you'd like. I have to report to Aegir on my mission. Depending on if he has another, it might take some time. You're also welcome to go back and rest."

She found she didn't want to waste her time inside. Even the little exploring she had done thus far had her itching to do more.

"I think I'll keep looking around."

She could appreciate the look of concern on his face before he nodded. At least he wasn't trying to tell her what to do.

Chapter Sixteen

Aby kept to the main road, dodging around children that were laughing and playing. She couldn't help but study everyone she came across. There were stories of women tending to home throughout history. It didn't seem there were any actual gender-specific roles here, though. She saw women and men both hanging clothes out to dry. They both were tending to the animals around their huts or scolding their children. The most striking moment was watching a man teach a young girl how to wield a sword.

"So you're the woman that Gunnar brought with him."

Aby hadn't realized she had been caught staring until a woman just a bit older than her approached from the other side of the fence.

"I didn't realize word had traveled so fast."

The woman shrugged, watching the man and child herself. "It's a small village, and we protect our own." Turning her attention back to Aby, she regarded her curiously. "I'm Gunilda. That's my husband, Leif, and my daughter, Astrid."

Aby froze for a moment, forgetting the name that Gunnar had given her. "I'm Thurid. I hope I haven't imposed on anyone by staying with Gunnar. I know he's probably well sought after."

Gunilda had gorgeous natural red hair. It wasn't like Aby had seen on boxed dyes back home. There was a mixture of colors that changed the hue depending on how the light hit it. She wore it long with braids placed throughout that Aby could never imagine being able to do herself. Catlike orbs watched Aby closely, studying her as if she weren't sure what to make of her. They were green that blended into a caramel brown. Her skin was kissed by the sun, tanned from her time spent outside. If anything, it showed that she wasn't afraid of hard work.

That made Aby like her instantly. She hoped the feeling would be mutual.

"Gunnar tries to keep to himself, but he's always fast to lend a hand when needed. We all want to see him happy and, if you're the one who can do that, all the better."

Aby wasn't sure she would be able to make anyone happy. At the same time, she could admit that she was jealous that Gunnar had so many people, even if he was oblivious to it.

"I'm glad he has so many people that care about him. Even if he doesn't realize it, he deserves more, but even I'm not sure he'll accept it."

The other woman leaned on the fence between them, grinning slightly. "Would you be willing to give it to him? The care and love he deserves, I mean."

Aby couldn't explain why she blushed, but there was something bold in this woman's gaze. It felt as if she were daring her to step further out of her comfort zone. She didn't know that Aby didn't belong here. She wouldn't be staying, and she didn't want Gunnar to get attached, only to leave him behind. That was too cruel.

"I think he deserves better than me. I don't have anything to offer him."

"There you are." Gunnar approached from the longhouse, offering Gunilda a smile. "It's nice to see you, Gunilda. How's Astrid's training going? Think she'll make a warrior yet?"

The other woman seemed to brighten up, her face friendly as she turned her attention to Gunnar. "Oh, she's giving her father quite a work. It'll at least keep the boys at bay. For a time, anyway."

"Well, send her my way when she wants to learn the bow. I'll have time for a bit to make her one of her own so it'll be ready." Placing his hand lightly on Aby's shoulder, he inclined his head. "If you don't mind, I'm going to borrow this one. I plan to start with teaching her some new skills."

Gunilda's grin seemed to convey baser thoughts of what skills she thought Gunnar meant to teach her. Aby could admit she had blushed more in a day here than she had in weeks in her world.

"You're giving them the wrong idea," Aby protested, following along as requested, though.

Gunnar glanced back at Gunilda, who watched them closely before shrugging. "Gunilda is known for having such thoughts. Besides, I think she's top of the list of people that want me to marry again."

Aby nodded thoughtfully, "She did want me to think about if I could make you happy, so I think she's pushing others towards it too."

Gunnar paused to look back at her, concerned. "Don't let anyone push you into something you don't want. We both know you aren't here for long."

"Actually, we don't know that." At Gunnar's look of confusion, she continued, "The rules of my mission are that I have to figure out and learn lessons in each world I go to. Until I learn them, I'm stuck in that world. I have no idea what the lesson could be for this world. I've been trying to figure it out all day."

He stared at her for a few moments before nodding, "Then it's even more important I teach you how to handle your own here. I can give you a place to stay until we build you a home of your own if you want."

Strangely, Aby didn't think she wanted a home of her own. She felt safer with Gunnar nearby, but she also didn't want to burden him. One day he would likely find a woman he wanted to start a life with. If she were still staying in his home, she would be in the way.

"You can start by teaching me what you think I need to learn. I can't promise that I'll stay in your home, though. If I am to be stuck here, I don't want to get in the way of your life. You deserve to have your bed back, as well."

He flashed her a playful grin, "We could always share it. Then we would both have a bed of our own."

The familiar burn resided in her cheeks once more. The sight caused Gunnar to throw his head back in laughter. It was a laugh that drew the attention of everyone around them and renewed the whispers once more.

Gunnar was true to his word. He led her back to his home, but instead of showing her inside, he headed back towards the structure he used as his stables. It seemed he kept some of his weapons in there. Or at least the ones he used for training. Vidar was still happily munching on the grass nearby, raising his head to meet their gaze before returning to it. She could envy his life.

"Try to pull this." Gunnar handed her a bow, watching her as she attempted to pull the string back. It was a little challenging, but she managed it. "That'll do for your training. It'll make you stronger as well."

She had done some archery back in a summer camp when she was in elementary school. For her journeys for archaeology, she had taken shooting lessons. She didn't carry a gun on her when she was on a dig site, but it was a good idea to be trained so she could help in case something happened. He draped a long, leather tube on her shoulder with a strap, the quivers sticking out the other end.

"These are training arrows. If you are here long enough, I'll show you how to make your own. We all have a signature on our weapons. It's how we can tell who the weapon was made by."

She couldn't help but glance at the arrows he gave her before looking at the ones he placed on his shoulder. The feathers were all black except for one strip of white. She wondered why he had chosen it as his symbol.

Gunnar led the way past his garden to the edge of the forest at the back of his home. There were targets set up lining the forest. It seemed this was something he was known for doing. She had strangely thought she might have been special. Then again, she had seen him offer to teach another how to use a bow and arrow.

"Have you ever shot one before?" Gunnar asked as a start. She nodded, preparing to nock an arrow to show him. "Good. Then this should be more of a refresher. You have good form. Lift your arm a little higher." He came up behind her, helping place her in position. "Perfect. Now you lightly touch the arrow to your lips, almost as if you are giving it your blessing to make its mark. When you're ready, let it fly."

She wasn't sure how she was supposed to be able to concentrate with him so close. He had already proven to be a distraction with his looks alone. The more time she spent with him, the more she found that she liked about him. She wanted to make him proud of her, though. Turning her attention to the task at hand, she pushed thoughts of him from her mind. Taking a deep breath in, she aimed for the target and let it fly. It wasn't quite where she wanted, but it did hit the mark.

"Did you see that?" It was ridiculous to get so excited when she had hit towards the edge of the target, but she had hit it nonetheless. Turning towards him, she threw her arms about his shoulders, jumping in her excitement. "I hit it! I figured I would miss the first few times!"

He chuckled, wrapping his arms around her waist to keep her from knocking him over. "I see that. Do you always get so excited over little things? You said you had done this before. It's not something you forget."

She hadn't meant to grab him in her excitement. She hadn't seen anyone else display affection so easily in the village. Slowly releasing him, she averted her gaze, feeling a blush color her cheeks once more.

"Sorry, I didn't mean to grab onto you like that."

He grinned at her, "I find that I don't mind you wanted to grab onto me in your excitement. You need to be able to trust me since I'm the one you were brought to."

That was one way to look at her situation. It was as if she were brought to him. Tilting her head to the side to study him, she wondered if he was connected to her lesson.

"Do you think you're part of my lesson?"

He blinked in surprise, furrowing his brow in confusion, "Why would I be part of your lessons?"

She wasn't sure, but it was the first time she was brought to a world in front of someone. If she hadn't already learned that she was capable of love because of her crush on Amun, she would have worried if that was what this was. Gunnar would have been easy to fall in love with. He challenged her to be more than she was and offered her protection and a safe space to be herself. Gunnar had made it clear that he had loved and lost and had no intention of loving again.

The god couldn't be so cruel as to offer her love in another world. How would they expect her to choose her world over love?

"You seem lost in thought. Is there something I'm missing?"

"No, I'm just overthinking. There's no way the gods would be so cruel." She offered him a smile before realizing they hadn't released each other yet. Clearing her throat, she stepped back with a shy smile. "I apologize for that. I get excited sometimes."

He motioned towards the target once more, "Let's keep practicing."

She lost track of how many times she nocked an arrow and sunk it into the target. It became a game between them to distract the other and see who overshot the mark the worst. That was how Aby found out that tough Gunnar was quite ticklish. She hadn't expected him to jump or yelp so loudly when she ran her fingers over his sides. It had been worth the mock glare he sent her and the promise that this was war.

As the sun dipped low in the sky, Aby was more than happy to call it. Her fingers had started to hurt from nocking the arrows so often.

"I think we can both agree I won." She grinned proudly.

"You only won because you cheated," he grumbled, gathering the arrows and storing them once more.

"Ah, my dear. All's fair in love and war."

He paused, turning a considering gaze to hers, "All's fair?" At her nod, he chuckled, "Then this is fair too."

Catching her off guard, he threw her over his shoulder. She gasped and yelped her own before laughing as he carried her into his home. Even the stares of the other villagers didn't dim her mood. This had been the kind of fun she had missed for far too long.

Chapter Seventeen

"Let me see your hands," Gunnar asked later that evening after they finished eating.

Aby could admit that she was full and content. It could have also been the ale that she had been nursing, but she was only slightly tipsy. It was enough to make her relax completely.

At his demand, she furrowed her brow, bringing her gaze to him. "Why?"

"I saw them while we ate. Let me see them so I can tend to them."

The skin wasn't broken, but they were angry and red from overuse. Holding her hands out towards him, he took them in his much larger ones. He spread some kind of ointment on them, working them into the skin carefully with a massage. She had never had her hands massaged before, but the heat from his hands seemed to activate something in the ointment that warmed and sent tingles into her injured hands.

"Would it be so bad for you to stay here, Aby?" She blinked her eyes open at his words, not realizing she had closed them. "You could have a life here that would be better than the one you had in your world. I think you would easily fit in here."

It was tempting. She couldn't count the number of times she had contemplated changing her name without telling anyone and starting over somewhere. This would have been even easier than that. No one would ever know who she had been or who her family was.

"What would I do with myself, though? You've found your niche in the world. I'm just a stranger who would have to learn how to fit in this world from scratch."

Silence fell once more as he continued to work on her hands. It was the same companionable silence that seemed to fill their silence. It wasn't something Aby was used to.

"Besides," she murmured, staring towards the fire, "I would only get in your way when you find a new wife. You and I both know the women of this village won't stop until you're married again. They think it'll make you happy."

He stared at her, his hands stopping their ministrations. That was what drew her attention to his.

"Why did you stop? Was it something I said?"

He shook his head before faltering and nodding. "You're right." It felt like a punch to the gut for him to agree that she would get in the way if she stayed. "They won't let me live out my days in peace until I marry again. They will if I marry again."

She blinked, pulling her hand from his, "If you already have a woman in mind, you shouldn't have let me stay here. It'll only make her angry."

He tried to suppress a grin but failed. "If I didn't know better, I would think you were jealous."

She shook her head sadly, "While anyone would be lucky to have you, Gunnar, we both know that I could leave at any moment. I wouldn't want to subject anyone to a life like that."

"And if you were who I would ask to be my wife if I had to marry again? Would you not want me?"

Their gazes met, both filled with uncertainty.

"What of love, Gunnar? We've only met. If I were to take a husband, I would want it to be for love."

"Do you not think you could come to love me? You said before that anyone would be lucky to have me as their husband. Were you lying then? Because I can assure you I could love you."

Aby was sure she had never been given such a fantastic compliment. If only her life weren't screwed up, she would have jumped at the chance to be with him.

"I wasn't lying then, but I don't want to promise you something that I can't keep. I don't know what the future holds. I don't know if I'll be here tomorrow."

He caught her hands in his when she made to push away from the table, stopping her. "No one knows that they have tomorrow, Aby. Life isn't a guarantee. You can either jump in with everything you have, or you stand on the sidelines watching. Which do you want to do?"

He was right. She had spent her entire life standing on the sidelines. She hadn't given her all to anything, aside from running from what she felt. If there was one thing that this journey had taught her, it was that even if she ignored it, the emotions were still there. She couldn't outrun them forever. Before meeting him, she hadn't been tempted as much as she was now. Even her belief that she was beginning to like Amun felt so small compared to this instant connection with Gunnar.

She felt the tears brimming her gaze; she met his, "Are you sure of this? You don't know me yet. There's so much about my past I haven't dealt with. Do you really want to sign up for a life with me?"

He nodded, offering a reassuring smile, "I'm sure. I haven't felt this alive in so long. You challenge me and push me to think outside the box. I want to learn more about you, but I'm all right with not knowing everything right now."

There was so much for them to cover, but Aby couldn't help the laugh that bubbled up. "This is crazy! If any of my friends back home had told me they were thinking of marrying someone the day after they met them, I would have called them crazy."

"It isn't so crazy here. Sometimes people don't even meet before they're married. We're ahead of the curve since we already like each other's company."

It was crazy. It was probably the most fantastic thing she had ever thought of doing, and she had spent most of her adult life on dig sites. She wanted him, though. Regardless of what happened tomorrow, she wanted to be with him.

"I don't think I'll regret saying that I would be honored to have you as my husband. I don't care if it were here or in my world. I don't think I could find someone that suited me as well as you do. You make life fun again. You make me remember that it's not just about throwing myself into work. I can laugh, and I can be goofy. What if I get taken away, though?"

Gunnar nodded, taking her question seriously. "I can't pretend I'm not worried about it as well. I will hunt down whatever god I have to that can bring me to you, though. Like you said, your world or mine, I wouldn't pick someone else to spend the rest of my life with."

"We can focus on the now until then." She squeezed his hands back, almost giddy with the idea of this decision. She had always heard stories of people meeting someone and just knowing. They had always seemed like fantasies. She could never wrap her head around meeting someone and merely knowing that they were who she wanted to spend her life with. Gunnar had been a surprise from the get-go. "What's the next move?"

He grinned, stealing her breath once again. "I'll notify everyone tomorrow. It'll take a few days to get everything together. They're going to want to throw a feast for us as well." Shaking his head, he gave a surprised laugh, "I can't believe you agreed to this. I thought I was crazy, and you were going to laugh at me."

She shook her head, chuckling alongside him, "On one condition, though."

"Anything. You just have to ask."

She blushed before nodding. "Kiss me."

Their gazes met, holding for what felt like an eternity. Gunnar released her hands before reaching out to cup her face. It felt so strange to ask to be kissed, but she wanted to make sure the chemistry between them was more than what they imagined. He leaned in slowly, giving her a chance to pull away if she wanted. She didn't want to, though. She didn't wait for him to close the distance. Leaning towards him, she couldn't help the gasp she released when their lips brushed.

It was soft, almost feather-light. He kept things that way, drawing out the moment for as long as he could. It wasn't enough for Aby, though. Wrapping her arms around his neck, she tilted her head to the side slightly. Brushing her tongue against his lips, she hadn't expected the groan that fell from his lips.

He crushed her against him, pulling her into his lap as he deepened the kiss. Their tongues battled each other, teeth clashing as the sparks they felt ignited into an inferno. It was more than she had expected. Finally breaking apart, they both stared at each other, panting.

"Well, that answers that question."

He grinned, shaking his head, "You're more dangerous than I thought."

"Or you've been out of the game too long."

Brushing her hair back from her face, he smiled softly. "I think I was just waiting for you."

Aby didn't want to lose this moment. She didn't want reality to crash back in. Curling closer to him, she rested her head on his shoulder.

"I guess you can move back into your bedroom."

They both chuckled, enjoying the comfort of each other's embrace and watching the fire crackle. Gunnar seemed content to sit there and enjoy her in his arms. Aby certainly did not incline to move. She felt she was a little crazy to want to be with a man she had only just met. She couldn't count the number of times she had laughed at people that claimed they loved someone they had only just met. She had thought them foolish and dreamers. Perhaps she was a dreamer now, too, though. She had lost herself to the past far too many years ago to be surprised that she would find love in the past.

"Did I ever tell you what the name I picked for you truly meant?" Gunnar's voice rumbled through his chest where her ear rested. She couldn't help but smile as she pulled back slightly to look up at him.

"You have my attention. What does Thurid mean, if not Thunder as you said?"

His grin was playful but shy as he answered her question. "It means Beautiful Thunder. You came into this world in a blinding flash of light, like lightning. Even though you were out of your element, you didn't back down. You stood your ground and were a warrior in your own right. It seemed too fitting to let it pass."

She blushed lightly, smiling softly up at him, "You thought I was beautiful even when I was half-drowned?"

He chuckled at her description of herself. "You didn't look half-drowned to me. You looked like you were ready to take on the world, and nothing would stop you. As I said, you looked like a warrior."

She didn't feel like a warrior, but perhaps he was right. She had dove into this journey headfirst. While she could have run or given up, she hadn't allowed herself to do anything but keep moving forward. No matter the setbacks, she had persevered. Perhaps she was a warrior, after all.

Chapter Eighteen

Aby hadn't slept so well in a long time. At least that didn't involve a full day's work in the desert's heat. There was something to say about feeling safe while sleeping that couldn't be beaten. Gunnar kept her close to his side in his sleep. She wasn't sure who was more surprised by how late they slept; her or him.

"Good morning," he grinned, brushing a kiss to her temple. "Are you ready to announce our decision to the rest of the village?"

Part of her wanted to stay in bed with him and ignore the world outside. That was the same world that could steal her away from him at any moment. Even so, it was the only way to get things moving towards their future as husband and wife.

"I suppose we should. Gunilda will be happy to know you won't be alone anymore."

Though she was sure, Gunilda would have rathered he ended up with someone from the village they knew. She wasn't about to let that happen now that she was here. He shifted away, pushing himself from the bundle of furs that had been their cacoon last night. While she knew she should get moving as well, she couldn't help laying there watching him. If anything, she owed Amun a thank you for this.

"You can stay there for a bit longer if you want. I'll let everyone know on my way for food. We'll probably want to eat in the main house for dinner tonight, but I wouldn't mind spending a little more time alone with you before it's taken away with plans."

He leaned down and gave her a lingering kiss, grinning when he pulled back. "I could get used to this."

She smiled brightly, stretching before flopping back into the furs. "I would like you to get used to it, too."

Watching him disappear out the door, she couldn't help the giggle that bubbled up. It didn't feel real, but she was going to take his advice. She was going to live for the moment, and, right now, he was the moment she wanted to live for.

"Well, isn't this sweet?"

She sat bolt upright in bed, staring at where Amun sat at the table. "No. You can't be here."

He flashed her a cocky grin, "Sorry to disappoint, sweetheart, but I'm here. And you know what that means."

It felt as if a hole had appeared in her chest. "You can't do this. Please, just leave me here. I want to stay with Gunnar."

Shrugging, he inspected his nails, "You agreed before you started. You had lessons to learn. You've learned them. Now you have to come back to the Temple for a final decision."

"I just told you my final decision. I want to stay here. I don't want to disappear on Gunnar like this. That would break his heart."

Amun shook his head, "No, it won't. He won't remember you."

The sob that tore from her throat felt as if it should have echoed across the world. She hadn't known her heart could break more than it had up until that moment. Her parents leaving her felt like a walk in the park at that moment.

"Please, don't take him away from me."

She didn't bother to hide the tears that streamed down her face. Staring Amun straight in the eyes, she begged to keep this. It was the only thing she wanted.

It seemed even Amun could be touched. He sighed heavily, shaking his head.

"My hands are tied on this one, kid. Naunet won't let you not complete this journey. You have to come back to the Temple. There's more to show you before you can make a decision."

"What more do I have to see? Haven't I seen enough already?"

He shook his head again, "You haven't seen what your world will be like without you. That's the last thing. Then you can make your decision."

She tried to hold back another sob as she nodded, "Can I at least say goodbye? I don't want him thinking I abandoned him."

Amun nodded. He could at least give her that.

"I'll return in an hour. If he hasn't returned for you to tell him you're leaving, I'm taking you anyway."

An hour wasn't much time, but Aby nodded anyway. He didn't have to give her that much. She buried her face into the fur, inhaling Gunnar's scent to try to imprint it in her memory. There was nothing written in stone that she would return to this moment or him.

"I brought everything we could need and then some. Apparently announcing I plan to take you as my wife has caused quite a stir and everyone wanted to give me something." He set everything down on the table before turning to where she still sat in bed. It took him only a moment to realize she was crying. "What's happened? Why are you crying? Are you re-thinking taking me as your husband?"

She shook her head, rising from the bed to throw her arms around his waist tightly. "I'm so sorry, Gunnar. I didn't know that this would happen."

His brow furrowed in concern before it dawned on him. "The gods came for you, didn't they?"

She nodded, burying her face against his chest, "They said I learned my lesson here. That it's time for me to go back and make my decision, they wouldn't accept that I wanted to stay here."

He held her tightly, brushing a kiss to the top of her head. "I will keep my promise, Aby. If they don't return you to me, I'll hunt down any god that will bring me to you. Your world or mine, it doesn't matter to me."

She wanted to believe those words, but the gods were known for playing games with what people wanted. She refused to release him, wanting to memorize this too. There was a chance she would never have such a moment again.

"I need you to know that regardless of what happens, this moment with you has meant more to me than anything in my life. For the first time, I don't feel like I'm hard to love." She pulled back to stare up at him, taking in his expression and features. "You are the man I have always wanted by my side. I wish it didn't take me traveling to another world to find you."

This time when Amun made his entrance, he filled the room with light. It was the best warning he could give. Gunnar turned to regard the man, pushing Aby behind him in protection. It only elicited a raised brow from Amun before he turned his gaze to Aby.

"I assume you're ready to go now?"

Aby shook her head before turning his gaze up to Gunnar. "I'm so sorry, Gunnar. I promise I'll try to find a way back to you."

She knew Gunnar wanted to fight for her, that he tried to pull her back to keep her from going with Amun. If there was one thing that Aby was famous for, she kept promises and commitments she had made. It didn't matter that she didn't want to anymore.

"Let's get this over with."

Amun offered her a soft, sad smile before turning his gaze back to Gunnar. He could respect how much the man wanted to protect Aby. She had made the right choice when it came to men. It was by far better than him. He gave the nod to Gunnar before taking Aby to the Temple.

Aby looked around the Temple before turning his attention back to Amun. "Okay, you brought me here. Now can you send me back?"

"I'm afraid you have to go through me for that. And there's much you have to learn before you can make that decision." Naunet stepped out of shadows that Aby didn't even know were there. Her beauty still struck Aby speechless, but she knew that Naunet held the keys to her future.

"What else do I need to learn?" It felt as if she had learned more in the last few days than she had in her entire life. "I thought this would have been enough by now."

Naunet nodded regally before motioning to the blank wall before her. "This is the future I'm to show."

"If it doesn't include Gunnar, I'm not interested."

She blinked slowly at her before sighing, "My dear, I hadn't planned to show you this, but since you insist. Allow me to show you Gunnar's future. You can decide if you love him enough to keep him or let him go."

Part of Aby didn't want to see this, but Naunet was right. Before she could make a decision, she needed to see all the details in play. The wall before her flickered like a movie screen before it showed the familiar yard she had spent hours in just moments before. Gunnar was a few years older, grey leaking into his hair. It was hard to discern it against the blonde, but it only made him look more distinguished.

He was chopping wood, going through the motions effortlessly. For a moment, he paused, glancing towards where Aby stood on the other side of the wall. She thought he was looking at her how his face lit up, but that thought was dashed mere moments later when a young girl ran towards him. She couldn't have been more than four years old. A little boy, a bit older, followed her, jumping into his father's arms. One more entered the scene, trying to pick up the ax their father had set aside. Gunnar threw his head back in a laugh before the final, metaphoric ax fell for Aby. A woman heavily pregnant came into the scene, waddling up to Gunnar to brush a kiss to his lips.

"He would have had a family without me there." Aby hadn't even realized that she had spoken out loud.

Naunet spoke softly from her side, "He would have met her in a few months. He would have rescued her on a mission, but now he waits for you. I think you know that he will keep his promise to search for you or a god that can bring him to you."

She nodded, swallowing against the knot that felt like it had fused in her throat. "I don't want him to cling to me. I don't want him to give up true happiness." She turned tear-filled eyes to Naunet, imploring her. "Make him forget me. I want him to have that happiness. I want him to smile like that."

Amun stared at her, sharing a glance with Naunet. He had made the right choice in choosing Aby. She was selfless. While most would have clung to the notion that the person would have been happier with them, Aby was willing to release him to find happiness without her.

"Even if it means you never find this love again?" Naunet pressed.

She nodded, wiping the tears from her cheeks. "Yes. He's been through enough. He shouldn't have to wait for me."

Naunet waved her hand over the screen, and the images disappeared. While Aby didn't want to deal with anything else at that moment, she knew Naunet wasn't done. She said she had futures to show her. There would be more.

"Would you like to see what happens if you choose your world?"

Aby wasn't sure she wanted to see it. When she left her world, she was being chased by Professor Sonstroem. She didn't want to know what happened if he caught her. There were some things she would prefer not to endure.

"Do I have to live it?"

Naunet shook her head, motioning towards the wall once more.

"Then show me."

Chapter Nineteen

The wall on the other side of the temple flickered once more with the film that was her world. It was strange to see herself in the third person, but she also knew she needed to see this. She had to make a decision that would affect not only her life but the lives of those she touched.

She was running through the desert once more, Professor Sonstroem gaining behind her. Baahir wasn't far behind him. However, what she hadn't seen when she had been running was that her screams had drawn others' attention from camp. She could make out Brandon and a few of the other workers following behind them. The workers had tools that could double as weapons.

"He didn't get to rape me," she said softly, her eyes riveted on the screen before her.

While Professor Sonstroem did catch her on the screen, shaking her as if he meant to shake sense into her, the rest of the group caught up shortly after and pulled him off. They dragged him away, Brandon offering comfort to Aby as they watched him taken away.

"You wouldn't have been harmed if you hadn't fallen in this Temple. Others are watching out for you." Naunet spoke easily, motioning to the screen before her. "Would you like to see what else your future held?"

Aby nodded, not sure if she would regret it or not.

"It isn't all happy; I'm sure you know. Life rarely is."

The images flickered again before changing to her sitting on the couch in her parent's home. She was wearing all black as people filtered in and out of the room.

"What happened?" she hesitated, asking.

"Your parents died in an airplane crash. They left everything to you, as expected. You became the head of their company."

She turned her gaze to Naunet, "They never tried to fix things with me?" At Naunet's head shake, she sighed heavily. "I guess I shouldn't have been surprised. They never really wanted me aside from having an heir to take over. Looks like they got what they wanted."

The truth was that Aby had no interest in her family's money. She never had. While she had allowed her parents to pay for her college, she had never bothered to get involved in the business. As soon as they found out she was going to school for archaeology, the money had stopped. In their minds, business was the only major that mattered. Everything else was a waste of time.

"This was the turning point of your life."

Aby glanced at Naunet in surprise. The death of her parents had been the changing point in her life?

"How would this be the changing point in my life?"

Naunet snapped her fingers causing image after image to flash by on the wall. Aby had taken over their company and changed it into something more. She did more for museums and antiquities, sponsoring digs that brought history to life. Because of her, the history of the world was improved. Her actions led to more people getting involved in anthropology and archaeology. It was more than she would have imagined happening in her life.

"What of love? Do I ever find it in my world?"

Part of her hoped that since Gunnar had found love without her in his life, she would also be able to find the same thing. Naunet sighed, shaking her head sadly, though.

"You dedicate your life to your work. You occasionally date men throughout your life, but your one true love will always be bringing history to life."

That much was accurate. Aby had always had a passion for ancient history. If even one person took up archaeology because of her actions, it would be worth it. Though, the truth was that she had now experienced what it meant to have someone want only her. While she wouldn't steal Gunnar's future from him, she wanted love of her own.

"I don't want either future."

Amun furrowed his brow, approaching her other side, "Is there another of the worlds you liked better? We can show you those as well."

She shook her head, offering them both sad smiles, "If I hadn't met Gunnar, I might have been satisfied with the future you offer. I have, though. I'm not selfless enough to give up the chance to have someone I can lean on by my side. Because of Gunnar, I want a family of my own. I want someone who will smile at me the way he will the woman he loves."

"So you don't wish to return to his world?" Amun hesitated in asking.

She did not doubt that he thought she would steal Gunnar's future from him. She could never do that to the man that had been willing to throw everything aside to help her. He deserved that happiness she had seen in his future.

"No, I want him to have that future you showed me. He deserves that and more. I just don't want to dedicate my life to making everyone happy with so little for myself." She laughed softly, grinning at them both. "If I had never traveled to other worlds and learned the lessons you taught me, I would have been willing to accept it."

Amun stared at her for a moment before throwing his head back in laughter. "I can't believe it. For once, I end up picking someone who doesn't follow any of the expectations."

Naunet scowled at him before turning back to Aby, "I can't promise that your future will be different. Every path alters with each decision you make. All I can do is allow you to pick a world that you wish to return to. You must choose one, though."

While a part of her wanted to go back to Gunnar, she had meant what she said. Gunnar deserved more than she could offer him. He deserved someone that was of his world. While she didn't want to go back to her world and continue enduring the life she had been, she knew it was the only life she could alter.

"Send me back to my world. I'll take my chances on being able to alter my future."

"Are you sure? Once you make this decision, it can't be undone, and you won't be given this chance again." Naunet didn't want her to make this decision lightly. Altering the future was never an easy one, even in the world she was meant to be in.

There was no point in pausing or hesitating. The only world that would have tempted her was with Gunnar, and that wasn't an option. Eliminating that ensured she had only one choice.

"Yes. Send me back to my world. I'll handle it from there." Pausing, she turned to both of them with a soft smile. "Thank you both, though. You've been wonderful through this. I don't think I would have been able to last this long if I didn't have either of you watching over me."

Amun offered her his characteristic grin before shrugging. "I can't pretend this hasn't been the most fun I've had in a long time. Thank you for that. I hope you get what you want from your world."

It was ironic for a god to be wishing her luck. He could have changed her future if he wanted, of that she was sure. Naunet seemed to keep him and the others in check, though. She wanted humans to make their own decisions in life. She could appreciate that.

"I wish you luck then," Naunet said softly.

A snap of her fingers put Aby once more in the desert at night. She could hear Professor Sonstroem yelling for her once more. While she knew now that others were coming behind him, the situation still made her blood run cold. She didn't hesitate to start running once more, wanting to put as much space between them. Knowing her future didn't make it any easier to endure.

"Abigail! You must stop! The desert is dangerous at night!" He called out to her.

She didn't bother to turn her attention towards him, merely kept running as she yelled. "I think I'll take my chances with the desert than fall into your clutches."

"I don't want to harm you! The gods have brought us together for a reason!"

"You've lost your mind, Professor! We weren't brought together for this! We were brought here to show the world the gods of Egypt still live! They want to be worshipped again, not to fulfill your dating desires!"

Having spent more than a few days with a couple of gods, she knew that Osiris was merely allowing Professor Sonstroem to believe that they were fulfilling his desire. Osiris didn't care about the man. He simply wanted to gain more power by being worshipped once more.

The silence stretched between them. Aby wasn't sure if it was because he was thinking over what she had said or if he thought she was just saying it. The silence hid the fact that he had gained on her. She hadn't realized how close he had gotten until he grabbed her, causing her to trip over her own feet and tumble to the sand once more.

He grabbed her shoulders as she had seen in the images provided by Naunet, shaking her roughly.

"You must see that we are perfect for each other, Abigail. You can't deny what the gods have placed before us."

"Let her go, Sonstroem!" Brandon's voice had a sob of relief falling from her lips.

Mere moments later, the men he had brought with him were pulling Sonstroem off her.

"Are you all right, Aby? I saw him approach you at the top of the dune before you struggled and ran. I'm sorry I didn't get here sooner. I wanted to grab reinforcements." Brandon helped her to her feet, inspecting her closely. "He didn't hurt you, right?"

His concern touched her, "You came just in time. If it hadn't been for you, I don't want to think about what might have happened."

"Let's get you back to camp. We'll have to figure out how to handle Professor Sonstroem, but at least we can make sure you're safe."

At least not everyone seemed to think she had done this to herself. Offering him a soft smile, she nodded though she stepped from his hold.

"I appreciate your help. I'll follow alongside you, but I think we both know it wouldn't do either of us any good if we showed up with your arm around me. I think I've had enough rumors to last me a lifetime."

<u>Chapter Twenty</u>

Aby wasn't sure what she expected when she arrived back at camp. Considering how poorly everyone had treated her before, she rather expected a cold reception. However, it seemed to have others come to your aide and stand up for you did a bit to change other's opinions. She went from being the girl everyone claimed was sleeping her way to the top to a victim of a crazy man in mere hours—at least mere hours for them.

The workers sent for the local authority. They wouldn't allow Professor Sonstroem's action to go unpunished. While everyone assumed the dig would be shut down, it seemed to find Osiris's temple entrance was enough to have their sponsorship transferred to another. While Aby wasn't sure she trusted Baahir to lead, she knew he would focus on the task at hand. He would ensure the temple was uncovered instead of focusing on romance.

It seemed Osiris would get his way, after all. She wondered how Amun was handling it. It was sad to realize she had bonded with the god, especially since she knew she wouldn't meet him again. While she was glad that the dig wouldn't be halted for the season, she found her excitement to continue the dig had died on her journey. She had had enough adventure for one year.

"Do you really mean to leave?"

Aby hadn't expected Baahir to speak to her of her departure. Since he had gotten the head of the dig, she imagined he had gotten all that he wanted. Osiris would be happy to have one of his loyal subjects in charge of bringing him to light once more.

Aby turned towards him with a soft smile, "I do. I think it would be better for all that I leave. Besides, we both know what happened here. I don't want to be involved in the games Amun or Oriris are playing with each other. It seems likely if I stay, it'll end up just that way."

Baahir seemed to consider that before he returned her grin. "This is true. While it can be exhausting to be at the whim of the gods, I wouldn't trade it for anything." Holding his hand out to her, it reminded her of how friendly they had been when this first began. "I wish you the best. I hope that whatever Amun showed you gave you hope for the future."

Hope for the future? She didn't want to think of it right now. She had to figure out how she was going to alter her fate to the one she wanted. Neither Amun nor Naunet seemed inclined to change it for her. Then again, she doubted she would have liked them involved. Sometimes the gods thought they knew what was best and ended up making things worse. Look at what might have happened to Gunnar if she hadn't stepped in.

Besides, with what had happened before, she doubted many of them would miss her. Her departure was quiet. Brandon offered her a hug and asked if she would return next year. She made no promises. It was time she started living for herself. She couldn't do that with her head stuck in the past. Jazz offered her a quiet apology for her actions, but they both knew their friendship wouldn't be the same afterward. Aby had trusted that she, of all people, knew her the best. Jazz had proven that to be incorrect when she had turned against her so easily.

She had plans for her next step, at least. It didn't involve working on another dig site somewhere around the world. She would return to the states and get herself an apartment before taking up a position at her parent's company. They would be happy to have her in their ranks. They would likely see it as proof that she had grown up and was ready to take on more responsibility. She hadn't been able to reach her parents, as expected. Instead, she had placed a call to their secretary. Mrs. Price had been more than happy to begin working on finding her an apartment that suited someone of her stature. She also promised to let her parents know to have a contract drawn up for her employment.

She spent the time she had waiting for her flight to research information on her parent's company. While she was part of the family, she hadn't bothered to worry about what they were doing. She was living her life, and they lived a separate one. If she meant to change her life now, she had to start somewhere. This seemed the best move.

Her parents were involved in many areas of the world, though they focused mainly on pharmaceuticals. She could remember her father stating that it was where the money was. Aby had always thought it was wrong to make money off of an illness or the death of another person. Remembering that Naunet said she used her power in the company to get involved in antiquities and spread history to the world, Aby had a plan to propose a new venture for the company. This would include working with museums and universities and an education program that brought the information to children worldwide. She didn't want anyone to be held back because of how they were born.

As strange as it was, she meant to make this proposal part of her agreement with them to join their company. Their family name was renowned by people in their circle. They were known by the rich and powerful. However, Aby wanted to sell making them known to the masses. It would include educators and countries far and wide. If she were going to get her parents to agree, it would have to play to their egos.

As she boarded the plane, she could admit that she would never have tried to do this if it hadn't been for the journey she had endured. It had taught her that she had a lot more she could do to change the world. She had been so focused on running from her past and the connections she could have used that she hadn't realized it. She wasn't inclined to repair the relationship with her parents. There had been too many missed opportunities for her to believe they could change and become a family. However, this was the means to be able to begin to change the world.

She worked for the entire flight back to the states. While she knew her family would have offered her the company jet to get around faster, she didn't mind the long flight that let her work. She needed as close to a concrete plan as possible to present them. If they turned away her ideas, she would have to find another route. Then again, if Naunet were to be believed, the company would be hers in a few short years. She didn't want anyone to die so that she could enact her goals.

As expected, a driver was waiting for her when she arrived. There was also an assistant that her parents had assigned her to ensure she kept on schedule. To be late was inexcusable to them. It didn't matter that she hadn't been late a day in her life. They wouldn't know that because they hadn't been around to see it. She shoved the thoughts that were clouded by the past from her mind. She needed to go forward with a clear head. It was the only way she would complete her plan.

"I am Brian McDowell. You may, of course, call me Brian, Miss Washington. Your parents set aside today to allow you to get settled. I've also been tasked with ensuring you have a proper wardrobe. Your parents have set you up with an apartment close to their main offices. I believe that will be to your liking."

She tilted her head curiously at the young man that had been assigned to her by her parents. It also meant that she knew where his loyalties were. She doubted he was much older than her. His suit was immaculate and tailored to fit him. He subconsciously unbuttoned the jacket as he sat, still going down the list of information she had no doubt Mrs. Price had provided him. His hair was a darker chestnut and held in place by more gel than she thought he required. Intelligent golden orbs met hers occasionally, a slight up-tilt to the corners that gave them an almost cat-like quality. He was a handsome man, but not something that would distract her. After all, her parents wouldn't want her falling for help.

"Please call me Aby, Brian. I assume we're going to be spending quite a lot of time together. I know that my parents pay you well, but I would like to think we can come to an agreement. I would rather you not report everything back to my parents." Turning her gaze out the window, she rested her chin on her fist with a sigh. "I have plans, you see. I want to expand the company into areas we aren't already. I want the companies name to be in the mouths of everyone. I can't do that if you're reporting every step to my parents." She turned her gaze to him, remaining serious, "I assume that your interest in this company isn't to be only an assistant, right?"

He gulped, set down his tablet to regard her. "I was told that you needed to be watched closely. They don't think you're serious about wanting to be involved with the business. Why should I believe you mean to expand this business in a way that would be beneficial for the company?"

She chuckled, offering him a friendly grin. "I like that you're protective of it. My parents made a good choice. You don't have any reason to trust me. Just as I have no reason to trust you, you'll have to take a gamble on this."

She didn't bother to answer any of his questions. The last thing she needed was for her parents to get wind of her ideas. She had to be the one to present them. Otherwise, they might implement them without her help. While it wouldn't necessarily be a bad thing, this was her future, and she would be the one to lead the change.

The rest of the afternoon was filled with going from boutique to boutique, trying on and buying clothes to be added to her new wardrobe. Corporate life meant she had to forego her usual khakis and tee shirts for suits and dresses. She couldn't remember the last time she had worn heels. Knowing it would be a painful transition, she also had Brain buy a foot spa she could use every night.

"Brian," she asked as they loaded back into the car to take her to her new apartment. "Do I have a fund for my apartment? I mean, for decorating."

Brian made a couple of taps on his tablet before nodding, "Yes, you have quite an extensive housing budget. The apartment is already furnished to ensure an easy transition, but you will be able to make any changes you wish."

That was a relief. She wanted her apartment to be her haven. While she knew her parents would like it to fit into their world, she doubted she would do much of any entertaining in her apartment. She barely noticed the time that passed to get to her new apartment. Brian had people waiting to carry her bags up to her apartment for her. She had no doubt they would have put it away for her if she hadn't intervened. Her parents might have control over a decent amount of her life, but she would control this space.

"Thank you for your help today, Brian. What time is my meeting with my parents tomorrow?"

"It is at nine am, Miss. Would you like me to have dinner brought up?"

She shook her head, "No, thank you. I'll figure something out. You may go. I'll see you in the morning."

It felt as if a weight were removed from her shoulders when they all left. She wasn't sure how she was supposed to get used to people always being in her day-to-day life. It was expected, though, to help keep her and her schedule on track.

Kicking off her shoes, she grabbed the bags from today and carried them to the bedroom. Everything here was as she expected; pristine and white. It terrified her to think of eating anything in the place. The site of the large bed was enough to make her realize just how tired she was. Glancing at the bags, she shrugged and dropped them onto the floor. They would be fine until tomorrow. Without another thought, she fell into bed, exhausted from the last few days.

Chapter Twenty One

Aby ensured she was ready ahead of schedule. She didn't need Brian or anyone else complaining about her. She tamed her hair into a low bun and made sure her makeup was tasteful but understated. The point was to ensure her parents and anyone else she would be forced to present before paid attention to her plans and not her. She wouldn't admit that she was nervous, but she was. After all, this was the first time she saw her parents since she was a child.

Brian rattled off what her parents had planned for her for the day. If her plan went the way she wanted, that schedule would change and be under her control. While she tuned him out, she focused on the information she had brought with her in the briefcase at her side. They would realize it was for the good of the company to expand into these fields. On top of that, the number of charity events they could hold to improve the company's reputation would be in their best interest.

The building that Washington Enterprises had bought to house their workings was one of the taller skyscrapers. The glass walls reflected the world around it outside but kept anyone from looking into the company's goings-on. Her parents were always worried someone would try to steal company secrets.

Brian led the way once more, offering greetings to people as they passed. Not once did he stop to make an introduction of who she was. Aby wasn't surprised, though. It seemed everyone already knew who she was before she had arrived. They kept their distance, speaking in whispers after she had passed. She would deal with that later. If she were working with this company, she would ensure that they knew she wasn't like her parents. There would be an open-door policy for her. They could come to her about any issues they may have had.

Her mother and father were as she remembered them. She got her coloration from her mother; the same blonde hair and blue eyes she saw in the mirror stared back at her. The difference came down to the emotion in those eyes. Aby saw hopes and dreams in the mirror. In her mother's gaze, she saw calculations and suspicion. She hoped she never had the same look in her eyes.

Her father's gaze seemed more bored. It felt as if he thought this was a waste of his time. She didn't quite remember what her father had looked like when she was younger, but his hair had turned gray over the years. She was somewhat surprised he didn't have more wrinkles, but she assumed the money would ensure they didn't show more than they wanted.

"Darling," her mother cooed, leaning on the edge of her father's desk. "It's about time you decided to join the family business. This meeting wasn't necessary, but we wanted to make sure you knew you were welcome here."

She inclined her head, making no move to cross to them as she was sure her mother expected. They weren't a family. They hadn't been a family in far too long. Aby meant for this to be a business arrangement that she started today.

"Thank you for allowing me the opportunity. I wanted to present you both with a concept that would improve the company's reputation. I know we've had a few scandals related to investments over the years. This would go a long way to change the public's perspective of Washington Enterprises."

Her father leaned back in his chair, shaking his head. "We have enough that we're working on at the moment. You were brought in to learn how the company is run. If you want a project, take one of the ones we've been working on."

She shook her head, setting her briefcase down and pulling the documents she had gathered this morning. "I have to disagree. We've made strides to improve our clients' reputation, but what about putting the name Washington Enterprises in the mouths of the general public? We work almost exclusively with the wealthy, but I know I would like to think of Washington Enterprises as the company everyone wants to work with. Small and large."

Once more, he shook his head, waving away her information. "If you want to make changes, you can do so when this company is yours. For now, you'll do things our way."

She sighed, nodding her head, "Well, then I guess I should take my ideas elsewhere. I understand if this isn't something Washington Enterprises would be interested in. After all, the charity work alone that we could do to help spread education to other countries is excessive. It would have meant having the first pick of the smartest minds out there, but, again, I understand if it's too much. Thank you for your time."

That seemed to get her father's attention and had him leaning forward once more. "What exactly is your idea? It's best if we hear it out before we throw it aside."

At least that much hadn't changed. Over the next hour, she laid out her plan step by step. She didn't just talk, though. After all, her father and mother had been in this business for a long time. Their knowledge would be crucial in ensuring her plans took hold. She couldn't lie that she was surprised they were so perceptive to the idea. It would need a little work, but she had the perfect idea of where to start.

"I thought I would reach out to the museum as a start. We need to get our names out there to encourage others to approach us."

Her mother frowned, "This seems like it would be more of a waste of money than improving things for Washington Enterprises."

"I can understand your concern, but I'm not talking about reaching out to the museum for us to give them money. I want to talk to them about using the museum for a charity event. It would open the doors not only to them but also for other events. Don't you want the next discovery made to have Washington Enterprises attached to it?"

She knew they would see the possibilities and avenues this would open for them down the road. They would be foolish to turn away from this even more so when she told them that she would head the project herself. They wouldn't have to expend anyone from their staff to take care of it.

"If we have an agreement, I'll place a call to the museum today to see if I can't meet with the curator. I'd like to get this started as soon as possible. It'll take more work to begin an educational side to the company, but it holds such promise for the future."

With their blessing, she left the office to find Brian standing outside.

"Perfect. Please show me to my office. I have a project to begin. And please get me the number for the closest museum. Any museum in the city. I'll call them all to find the perfect location."

Her office was just as she expected. Her parents were all about keeping up with appearances, after all. Her office resided on the corner of the building, a corner opposite her parents. It gave her quite an impressive view of the city. Her desk was a large mahogany executive desk with two leather chairs facing it for company. On the opposite end of the room was a couch with a coffee table before it.

"Here are the numbers you requested." Brian made quick work on his assignment.

There were quite a few museums to pick from, but her interest was in history. Her first call went directly to the Museum of History. She didn't believe she would get a meeting with the curator for her first choice, but Naunet made it very clear this was her path. She almost felt giddy over the whole thing.

"Yes, hello. My name is Abigail Washington. I work with Washington Enterprises. We wondered if we could set up a meeting with your curator about hosting an event at the museum for charity." The woman on the other end didn't know who Washington Enterprises was. "I understand that he's likely swamped, but if he could perhaps spare even fifteen minutes of his time, I would be more than happy to begin the conversation at least."

"Well, he does have about twenty minutes between lunch and his next meeting. I don't suppose you could get here by 12:30?"

Aby glanced at the clock, noting it was 12:15 already. It would be tight, but she wasn't going to pass up this chance.

"I'll be there. Thank you so much."

Grabbing her briefcase, she barely spared Brian a glance. "Let's go, Brian. We've got a meeting at the Museum of History. Move quickly. I don't want to be late."

<u>Chapter Twenty Two</u>

The Museum was just as she remembered it. She loved getting lost in the halls here, surrounded by so much of the rest of the world. The curator's assistant had gone to find him while Aby wandered the halls. She told Brian he could take his lunch while she worked. She wanted to have a conversation with the curator without external ears. This event would have to be something that both Washington Enterprises and the Museum would benefit from.

"Well, I daresay this is a surprise."

Aby spun around in shock to see Amun standing not far from her. "What are you doing here? I thought I wouldn't see you again."

It was nice to have a friendly face as she worked to start her new life. She barely stopped herself from offering him a hug. Was it proper to hug a god? This was unfamiliar territory for her.

"I wanted to check on you. I find I was concerned at how you would handle this transition." She grinned, earning a frown from him. "Don't get used to it. I guess I found you rather interesting. I know this isn't what you wanted, and I feel horrible about what happened with Gunnar."

Her expression dimmed at the mention of his name. "Did everything happen as it should have for him? Did he forget me?"

Amun nodded, "It did. He met the woman that you saw and had five beautiful children. You saw a few of them in the vision."

"Perfect. I'm glad it worked out."

He glanced around the Museum before smiling at her, "Couldn't stay away from history, could you? I thought I might find you here. What brings you here, anyway? And dressed so professional."

She gave him a small spin to show off the new suit before shrugging, "Phase one of my plan to change my future. I'm here to meet with the curator about using the Museum for future events. This way, I can immerse Washington Enterprises into the world I love."

"I certainly don't want to get in the way. Best of luck. I'm sure we'll be seeing each other very soon."

Aby assumed he would have disappeared as he used to, but he simply meandered down the hall, looking at the displays.

"I am so sorry for the hold-up. He should be here in a moment." Aby gave the assistant another smile, nodding her understanding.

Once more, she turned her gaze to the walls around her. If this worked, her escape from reality would once more be a part of her life. Even though so much hung in the balance on this meeting, she felt at peace within these walls. She might make a point of coming here daily.

"I'm so sorry I kept you waiting. I had an important phone call to take. Miss Washington, correct?"

Aby turned and barely kept her mouth from falling open in surprise. The man walking towards her briskly looked exactly like Gunnar, though his hair was cut shorter and styled. A part of her wanted to turn back to see if Amun had anything to say about this, but she had more important matters at hand.

"Yes, that's me. Are you the curator?"

He chuckled, his grin less guarded than Gunnar's had been. "Not quite. The curator is actually out getting some antiquities. While he's gone, I take charge. I'm Ethan Merrick." Aby shook his hand, unable to believe this was happening.

"Have you worked here long, Mr. Merrick?"

He shook his head, "Not quite. I came here around a year ago. Why do you ask?"

She waved the question off, reminding herself to focus on the task at hand. "Nothing. Nevermind. Shall we go over my ideas for a charity event here? I would like for Washington Enterprises to be more involved in antiquities and history. If we don't learn from the past, we're only going to repeat it."

Ethan nodded his head, that killer grin spreading into a full smile. "I'd love to hear what you have in mind. If you would follow."

Aby couldn't stop herself from glancing back towards where she had last seen Amun. He gave her a wink before finally disappearing. The gods just loved to play games, didn't they?